P9-CBG-481

ALSO BY ROBERT OLMSTEAD

A Trail of Heart's Blood Wherever We Go
River Dogs
Soft Water

AMERICA BY LAND

AMERICA
BY LAND

ROBERT OLMSTEAD

RANDOM HOUSE ▪ NEW YORK

All rights reserved under International and
Pan-American Copyright Conventions. Published in
the United States by Random House, Inc.,
New York, and simultaneously in
Canada by Random House of
Canada Limited, Toronto.

Library of Congress Cataloging-in-Publication Data

Olmstead, Robert.
America by land / Robert Olmstead.
p.   cm.
ISBN 0-679-41130-5
I. Title.
PS3565.L67A74 1993
813'.54—dc20   92-50511

Manufactured in the United States of America
24689753
First Edition

For Cindy

And you won't leave soon
because I know
You're just like me
with no place to go

And there's a love still here
No, nothing's died
It just got hurt
And buried deep inside

"Inside," by Bill Morrissey

ACKNOWLEDGMENTS

The author wishes to thank Amanda Urban and David Rosenthal. Their conviction and constancy means more than they will ever know.

AMERICA BY LAND

1

There is a true story about a woman in New Mexico and a boy riding out to see her. It goes like this: He's riding a big American motorcycle from Pennsylvania, from New York State, from wherever he's been, and as he rides he thinks, Nobody knows me like she does, nobody. She's his cousin and he misses her sorely. They haven't seen each other for some time now. He's thinking about the weighing of time, the missing, the leaving behind.

★

She's wearing a skirt she sewed together from her father's neckties. Most are striped and paisley silk; some have whales on them. Not the phony kind with fatheads, fuming spouts and curled flukes, but real whales, sperm, pilot and killer, whales that rise up to her hips when she spins in place and settle back down around her ankles when she stops.

But she doesn't spin in this heat, this air that fills the lungs like warm talc. She dabs at her neck and cheeks and forehead and gives up, letting the sweat trickle to between her breasts and under her arms and down the insides of her legs. She didn't grow up here. She grew up where it was cool and green and breezy, the wind soothing the trees or freighting snow, and out beyond, the deep, sonorous ocean.

She waits for him at the sink, under the pale dead moon that takes up the night sky. He's riding in from the East Coast. She lets herself think, This is how it is with women, always waiting at the sink cooling their blood from a point at the wrist where the water crosses, listening to it guzzle, while with men, they're always coming or going, coming or going. They are so busy.

She waits for rain, too, and when it comes it'll thump the earth like small hooves, making splashes of dust, then going to mud. She shuts off the faucet and, barefoot, pads quietly over the cool square tiles. She goes to the room where she sleeps, unbuttons the skirt and lets it drop to the floor. She lies down and thinks about rest, thinks about forgiveness.

She's in the days of longing, longing fixed like the hands of grief at her throat. Breathe, she reminds herself. Breathe. Breathe. Breathe. It's okay. It's okay for now.

★

He pulls over in Glenrio, New Mexico, for gas and coffee and decides to try some breakfast. He's some days out. He was supposed to be in college, but quit and took a job in a quarry. He had no business in school. He's twenty-three and doesn't like being told what to do. When he quit school, he headed north to Connecticut to see Juliet and found out she'd left for New Mexico. So now he's going to where it's clean and unfertile, where it's dry, where he's the only standing water on the land.

★

The woman. She's up and walking around, touching the adobe walls, holding her stomach as if she were still pregnant, but she hasn't been that way for a while.

She feels hollowed out. She had something in there but now she doesn't.

The adobe is for sale. The furniture is covered with white sheets. The sign out front says BETTER HOMES. What does that mean? She wants to kill the sign painter and cut him up into little pieces. The idea of men makes her cringe. She shakes because she's frightened herself. Where's Redfield when she needs him? She wonders, Was I the baby or was I the mother? She wonders, When is this? Is it tomorrow already?

★

Eggs, sunny-side up, with a flour tortilla. He's tired and when he gets tired he takes to staring, falling off within himself, down and down and down. He shifts in his chair, trying to wake up, to get comfortable. He's been riding a long time and his ribs are killing him. They're wrapped in white bandages from where he got pinned between two loaders down in the quarry. They gently squeezed until he wanted to die, but he kept his mouth shut so the flicker that is life could not escape.

★

You know this story and want it to be about you. You want it to be you.

2

When Juliet came west, she brought her grand-mother's gateleg table. She dismantled it and carried it in a garment bag. There wasn't room for much else and she didn't mind. She was alone and eight months' pregnant, flying to Albuquerque to give her baby up for adoption.

She now thinks about that table stacked in a corner as she stirs the chili con carne: meat, beans, onions, peppers, chili powder, cayenne, chilies, cumin, oregano and garlic. Her cousin Redfield is coming her way and he'll be hungry. He called her number from somewhere on the road. He said he was bound for Poteet but missed his exit.

He said, "Juliet?"

She said, "Yes."

He said, "It's me, Redfield. I'm coming."

She said, "Hurry."

Maybe Redfield can put her table back together. He is so good with his hands. When her grandmother gave her the table, she said, Don't hold on to anything too tightly because you might find yourself leaning on something not attached. But this, this is a good table.

After he stood her up, her fiancé said, May you have a golden dawn and a tranquil future.

Before she left for New Mexico, her father said, Having a daughter is like a needle in the heart.

When Redfield gets here she'll mother him. She'll make him eat a lot of garlic. Garlic contains several volatile sulfur compounds. It will lower his high blood pressure, reduce his serum cholesterol. She doesn't know he's been injured, doesn't know he quit school. It won't matter. She needs him here right now.

The smell of the chili makes her whoozy. She's just coming off a seven-day fast. She wanted to cleanse her being. Her last meal was a cashew.

On the radio they're playing Patsy Cline, "Crazy" and "I Fall to Pieces." When Patsy Cline died, Juliet was born. After Martin Luther King, Jr., died, Redfield was born. Juliet thinks Patsy Cline hung the moon and stars, and every time she hears the "I Have a Dream" speech, she starts to cry.

She looks out the window, tries to see the curve of the

earth. It's not there today, not where she remembered it to be. Maybe it will be there tomorrow.

Her period is late. It's been late for ten months now. The fast and being pregnant didn't help much. Besides, she heard where all the tampons were shipped to Saudi to plug bullet holes. Much faster than a bandage. They should be home by now.

"I think I'm discovering what my problem is," she whispers. "I think I'm a plant. I'm ectopic or whatever the hell that is. I grow towards the sun."

She looks around the room, looks for her voice, touches back her hair. She feels faint so she lets herself down onto the cool floor, onto her stomach, her cheek pressed against the tiles. She can see into the bottom cabinet where a box of cereal has tipped over and corn-flakes are scattered on the shelf. She begins to feed herself one flake at a time, tasting them, melting them, then swallowing.

She tries to remember the last time she saw Redfield but it's difficult. Giving birth has a way of ending old history with the prospect of a future. Now she has neither history nor future. She's where she is, moment by moment. She thinks, If memory is heaven, this must be hell.

Outside is the mountain. Warm updrafts build towers of clouds miles into the sky. Over the high ridges, thunderheads generate pyrotechnic lightning. Sometimes the mountain wears a garland of clouds, a crown of clouds. And down here is the tiniest bit of rain. Out here the air is not translucent; it's transparent. At night the mountain goes the color of watermelon.

"I'm much too young to feel this damn old," she says, savoring another cornflake, beginning to like the echo of her voice.

She sighs, then smiles with an idea. She reaches under her T-shirt and finds a nipple. She rolls it between her thumb and first finger, pulls and squeezes. She wets her hand and licks the sweet milk from her fingers.

Redfield will be here soon. They can catch up on each other's lives. They'll say, Howdy do and How ya been. She thinks, When Redfield gets here everything will be better.

She reaches under her shirt again and this time falls asleep, holding her breast.

★

Redfield shuts down the Harley and steps out onto the desert. He's never been here. He's spent his life in the northeastern forests, where the earth is black, the loam thick, and the land bulges with rocks like knuckles. But this land runs on before him, immodest in its disregard for limitation. It's like the ocean or the maximum northern winter. This isn't a place for weak minds.

The desert says, Fuck with me and your life is forfeit.

In 1948 his father passed this spot. He and a friend left the dead cold of New York State for the promise of southern California. His father was eighteen, without much money, but his friend was flush. He'd just finished a hitch in the army and could lay down the six hundred for a brand-new used Nash.

His father wanted to be an artist, but now he's a little bit wealthy, gone a little bit crazy as they say. He drinks his coffee with Borden Eagle Brand sweetened condensed milk. He has cluster headaches and worries about electromagnetic fields. He watches public TV shows about men who share their feelings. Men in parts of the country gathering to do this. Men across America sharing their feelings for the first time. Christ, how desperate can you be?

Redfield's weariness goes bone-deep. It creeps into every joint, chews at every muscle. His mind is blank with the heat of pain, a great yawning ache, but he's wide awake. He's looked into the flame. He has welder's eyes. He's on the road his father was on.

He fixes on the sunflowers along the median. America, he thinks, God's golf course and this is his sand trap.

Last night Redfield lay awake and asleep in the inky darkness, needing some rest, not trusting himself on the motorcycle. He tried to get a room in Amarillo, but there weren't any. In the morning he awoke to black-eyed Susans, pine trees, short and squat and round and black. The earth had turned to red, with outcroppings of boulders, sand filtering between. There were tufts of weepy trees, pinkish and dusty looking at the tips. Where have I come to, he wondered. And then like memory he was in the sere desert, running the edge of the horse latitudes.

Juliet is waiting for him in Corrales. Something is

wrong and he doesn't know what. He makes himself get back on the Harley and pushes the run to Tucumcari. Whole miles stretch out before him and he can see where he'll be a half hour from now, cresting the horizon, entering the highway's vanishing point. There's a temptation to step off the bike and into the transparent air, run alongside for a while. You don't get many chances like this in life.

He's glad to be in New Mexico, to be outside the helmet, hair snapping back behind him, the wind and sun burning his face, his motion through the still air making its own blow, knifing through this piece of atmosphere.

Ahead is Tucumcari Mountain, long a landmark for travelers along the Canadian River. Pedro Vial mentioned it in 1793 while opening a trail between Santa Fe and St. Louis in order to find the best route from Arkansas to California. Captain Randolph P. Marcy led an expedition past here in 1849.

Redfield reads all this on a sign. Seems he remembers Ronald Reagan was either on that trip or in the movie. He thinks how the Apache must have been tickled pink.

At breakfast in Glenrio he allowed himself a taste of Old Black Dog's chicken powder, a maintenance hit. He let it melt on his tongue and it was like hard water out of a rusty pipe.

He thinks he needs to be coming down soon. Such thoughts make him feel he has his sanity on a string, but he still couldn't eat and even though he wasn't thirsty, he forced coffee and juice and water. He worries about dehydration. He remembers the story his father tells about his great-aunt falling through a floor register when she was eighty-four. She lay tangled in the duct work for two days with broken legs before she was found, only to die in the hospital of dehydration a week later. Sometimes it happens like that.

The pain in his ribs is now something different, something that follows him around, curious about his ways, bumping into him when he stops.

When he almost got crushed in the quarry, his foreman, Ronnie Dove, told him to keep quiet about the accident and they'd put him six months' wage.

"Give it all to me now," Redfield said. "In cash and I'm history. In cash and I make like a ghost."

"You say shit and the Ironheads go."

Redfield laughed. He wouldn't say shit. He liked the Ironheads. It was Big Ironhead and Little Ironhead, a little hopped up while operating the loaders what pinched him. Big Ironhead is the father and Little Ironhead is the son. Big is little and Little is big and that's how they got their names. They were his friends. It'd been an accident, one too many.

"Get gone," Ronnie Dove said at the time. "Meet us in Poteet, August first, or your ass is grass."

Fuck Ronnie Dove. In Poteet they'll clear right of way for a power line, hundreds of miles through condemned land.

So much to think about in this life.

He's running I-40, running in the bed of old 66 somewhere between Santa Rosa and Moriarty. He can see for ten miles. Again he gets that strange urge to step off the bike. He pulls over. He hands the Cowboy Junkies into the Walkman and wants to feel serene. He climbs dusty boulders, yellow desert poppy and lupine in the crevices.

He sits and forgets for a while he's injured, could be dying. He saw the same thing happen to John Wayne. The Duke got crushed. It was just made up, a movie thing. But the blood looked real enough. Strange how comforting thoughts like that can be. Especially for the young and the old, people who haven't had much life and people who've had their fill.

He watches the cars on the interstate, listens to the trucks do the Doppler. He picks at a callus with his knife. The motorcycle is pulled off, tucked away. He can see it. The motorcycle is a compass pointing west. Juliet is waiting. She'll make it all better. She is light. She has all the answers. Wide awake, he dozes in the later sun, dreaming the color green, slipping into a speed sleep. He thinks about the library books he has left behind, overdue.

"They'll track you down," he mumbles, and then he tips over, falling off this rock and onto another.

3

In the evening the sunlight scatters away most colors
so all that's left is reddish hues. She's past the white
trailer down a red dirt road, white trees suspended
whitely in the dead air and dry on the stump. The road
turns from red to black to red.

She's sitting on a bench by the open door, her legs
spread and her skirt a hammock of daisies, tiers of turquoise, red, lavender and green rayon. She feels better
after having something to eat. She bought this skirt in
Albuquerque and another one, blue and mustard with
gold metallic ribbon work, and another one, black chif-
fon with roses outlined in gold.

She dreams he's riding a rocket ship, erasing the world in his wake. He's riding in from Oklahoma. He heard of a job in Poteet but missed an exit a state ago and now he's coming on. He's coming her way like radio, like microwave, like X ray. She wants to be dreamy for a while, wants to be the kind of person who makes it all up. Wants not to cry.

In that same moment she sees and hears Redfield coming down the dirt road on his motorcycle, horses of red dust boiling up behind him, and he's there, stopped in her yard.

He straddles the bike, left hand on left thigh, right forearm on right thigh. His black hair is plastered back against his skull like a duck bird and his face is red and burned, mottled as if an abrasion wheel had drifted over it. The engine clicks and ticks as it sends feathers of heat to cool between his legs. His body tweaks. They stare at each other, smiling, starring in their own lives. She thinks he's a vision risen up from the bosque, and he thinks she's the true blue Madonna herself, her hair gone white in the sun, hair like sunspots, like pollen unclipping in the wind, hair like milkweed silks.

"Hey, pretty baby," he says. "I'd have been here sooner but I got lost on the eastern seaboard."

"Redfield. You are the A number-one bona fide asshole of the whole world."

"What a moment. Who needs the flicks?"

"Not I."

"I have come from the promised land," he says. Bethlehem and Nazareth, PA. I can feel the truth of God's light shining on me."

"That's good because I for one am desperately in need of lies."

"I'll lie to you later. I need sleep now," he says. "I've been up for days. I'm wicked tired."

She gets her shoulder under his arm and like drunks they go through the open door, through the living room, down the hall and to the bedroom, her bare feet padding quietly, his boots thumping and scuffing, his boot chains jangling. She backs him down onto the bed and begins to unzip, unbutton and unbuckle him. Inside his clothes she gets to the white sweat-stained bindings, takes in her breath and backs away. His eyes are open, but she can't tell if he sees. She tugs off his boots and lets them drop.

"I got banged up a little before the trip, but I came anyways. I'd have been here sooner, but I didn't learn to tell time until the eighth grade."

"How did you do it?"

"No sweat," he says, clenching his teeth. "It just came to me one day waiting for the bus."

She shakes her head and rolls her eyes, then drags off his jeans.

"I think I have to piss."

"The bathroom's in there."

"No. Outside. Help me."

The fat-bellied moon, now in all its fullness, is cradled in the black spindles of trees, just so much weight floating in the blue-veined sky of the night. They're stark white and where their skin is bare it prickles in the heat, sweat dances to the flesh. Out here, each star is a pool of water.

He walks slowly, his arms close to his sides, not moving them for fear their sway will make his ribs go to hurting. He can't imagine ever being on the motorcycle. He can't imagine being off it in this place where the rocks have gone to dust and the sand is fine like black powder. He thinks for a second, A match could set the whole thing off, and then he tells her again he has to piss.

"So piss," she tells him.

"I think I hurt my ribs again. I can't reach down. I stop moving, I get stiff."

She doesn't say anything. She comes up behind him, puts an arm around his waist and reaches down to hold him straight. They wait for a long time. She can feel his belly working. She closes her eyes and holds him while he pisses red into the ocher dust.

"That's a nicens tinkle," she says.

"I think I'm dying," he says, working his teeth, and they both break to laughter.

She says, "Sometimes, Redfield, you are so fucking cool."

They go back inside and Redfield lies down. She lies down too, rolls into him and disappears her head inside his arm. His jaw aches from clenching. His body sings like a wire and slickens with sweat, but he knows he'll be coming to rest soon. The swamp cooler hums. It says, Wet air is cool air.

Juliet is talking. He can hear her words, distant and distracted, as if coming from inside his chest.

She's saying, "I don't want to go back where it's so green. I want to stay here where it's brown and tan and white. I like it here where you are the only thing between earth and sun. I'm a big fan of the sun."

"No going back," Redfield mumbles.

"You are wonderful," she says. "You are so kind. You are handsome. Your touch makes my knees weak," and then they are both asleep, spent for the time.

That night a great bank of fog spills from the ridges of the Sandia, unfurling an opaque wall that looms a thousand feet higher than the ten-thousand-foot crest, a cataract of mist.

That night he dreams he's tired. Dreams he's riding, dreams about his friends: Old Black Dog, Little Ironhead and Big Ironhead. They're in El Paso at Old Black Dog's trailer, sitting around a pile of thrusters and rippers, pure Texas grit. Old Black Dog is telling them when he retires he's going to Soweto and fight in the revolution, kill white boys much like themselves. He was in Korea, Vietnam and Angola. The Ironheads say they want to go too, but Old Black Dog tells them they can't and they're disappointed because they have a lot of guns and are good shots. Later, Jimmy Carter comes by and they all build a house. When the house is finished, Redfield goes inside and finds his father sitting alone in the dark.

Jesus Christ, he says. What are you doing here?

His father says, If you sit in the dark long enough you can see everything.

Still asleep, Redfield determines he'll remember this dream, but he's too tired, out too long, and forgets it altogether. Juliet forgets her dreams too, after long and serious consideration.

★

In the morning, she'll make breakfast. He'll tell her it's his second breakfast in a row.

She'll tell him that was two days ago, drop a tortilla into the skillet and say, "A Woman in Las Palmas fried the image of Christ into one of these."

"Jesus was way cool," he'll say.

She'll stare into the black iron so as not to miss anything just in case the good Lord comes to her this morning. For her, these things still hold water.

"Two days ago?"

"Two days ago. You've been sleeping for two days."

She'll be mostly naked from the waist down and he'll watch the backs of her legs, the way they muscle when she moves, the way her ass flexes and dents when she shifts her weight. In his eyes, she's a diamond, long-legged and coltish, slow and languorous. He's still young. He still thinks this way, giving himself up to such old notions about love and women, harboring these thoughts as if they were fugitives from the law.

But for now he sleeps like a dead man, the movement of his chest so subtle and Juliet's fears so great that she comes out of sleep to prod him, to test him like a doctor. He sleeps deeply and with resolve not to move, not to make himself hurt.

4

When Redfield left Connecticut, he still hadn't made up his mind to come west. He only wanted to survive I-95 South. Passing into New York, he told the guy in the tollbooth, "You got balls charging people to ride this road."

"Tell me," the guy said. "I wouldn't ride this road if you paid me."

"What do you mean? I pay you and you're on this fucking road."

Behind Redfield, a horn blew and high beams flashed.

"Oh yeah. I guess you're right," the guy said, and then he ducked down, disappearing inside the booth.

Redfield figured he was pushing buttons and the police were descending on him that very minute.

Then he got lost. He was dreaming his cousin Juliet left her boyfriend and came to the farm in Conquest. It was summertime and he was there. They stood on the porch and looked at each other. It was a dream he kept playing until finally he was somewhere in Pennsylvania.

Connecticut had been a bust. Juliet's ex-boyfriend said she'd left to go to New Mexico to learn to make jewelry. Yeah, yeah, Redfield kept saying.

"Tell her I love her," the guy said.

"Yeah, you love her," Redfield said.

At a truck stop, he pulled in and parked the bike near the door, where he could keep an eye on it. The lot rumbled with trucks at idle. Big overhead spots opened the night with noise and wattage. Inside, it was quiet and all the tables were taken, so he drew a coffee and sat with a lone black man at the counter.

"Can I help you?" the black man said. He said *hep* for help and Redfield liked him for that.

"Nah. I was just going to sit here," Redfield said.

"What do you want?"

"Well, I'm beat and getting tired. Can't keep my eyes open."

"You got to watch that coffee. It'll poison you."

"I feel it. Did you know Coleridge drank eighty-four cups of coffee a day."

"Shit. Must've had a iron gut."

"He had dreams he turned into poems."

"I'll bet he did. Probably had a stainless steel touch-hole too."

"They didn't have stainless steel back then."

"They've always had stainless steel, kid, ever since the world began in nineteen-twentysomething."

"You got far to go?"

"If I lived here, I'd be home."

"Can't keep awake," Redfield said, looking away. "What do you trucker men do?"

"Well, kid, there's a lot you can do. Sleep. Avoid big meals. Go for high protein. Don't drink but coffee. Cup of coffee will stay with you for three hours. Wear loose underwear, wiggle around, dim your instruments, stop every hour. Avoid antihistamines, sedatives, Valium, tranquilizers, antidepressants and milk."

"Milk?"

"Milk will put you to sleep. Give them big rigs a wide berth 'cause there ain't nobody can contain them. Look out for them. Law say you supposed to sleep four hours for every eight hours on the road."

"What do you do?"

"Take me white crosses and think about rail-thin women with big beautiful butts."

Redfield nodded and sat back. They watched the truckers come and go.

After a while, the black man beckoned and Redfield followed him to his rig. It was a shiny black Kenworth with *Old Black Dog* on the door in script.

"Wait here," Old Black Dog said, going round to the back.

When he appeared again, he handed a bag into Redfield's pocket.

"Aren't you taking a chance here?" Redfield said.

"I saw you in Connecticut. Heard about you giving that man shit at the tollbooth."

"How do you know it was me?"

"I know everything. I see you."

"My name's Redfield. What's yours?"

"Could be Dog. I've sniffed enough assholes."

"I'll see you, Dog."

"No. I don't think so. I'm already gone. Already in old El Pass Assho holding my baby like chicken wings."

Lightning flashes quaked the horizon; eddies of light shivered against the black clouds. I am pleased to be here, he thought, to share this evening with Old Black Dog.

He stepped back as Old Black Dog ascended the ladder. They didn't look at each other again as the brakes chuffed and the tractor jogged forward, lurching against its load, hauling it to the ramp.

When Redfield crossed the Susquehanna it was near midnight. He rode the interstate to his exit and up the dark streets to town, to campus. He went into his dorm, where he still had a room, and lay down. He tried to sleep, but Old Black Dog's speed drove him like an engine. In the hallway there was noise. A frat party had run its course and now freshmen were wandering home more than a little drunk. They filled the hallway and were making much too much noise. He thought he heard his name and then he was sure he did, again and again. He was a mystery to them, a little older and private. They thought about him and talked about him, but he didn't want to be in their lives, no way, nohow.

He went to Henry's trunk, where he knew there was a bottle of Johnnie Walker. Henry was his roommate and a narcoleptic. He took mouthfuls of liquor until it was like water to him. The hall was still noisy and getting worse. He rolled a joint from Henry's stash, trying to put himself on the even. He heard his name again. He had to do something, because every time it got said it felt like a fishhook.

He pulled Henry's Dunlop Jumbo Driver from his golf bag and filled his jacket pockets with golf balls. The joint in his teeth, he stepped into the hall, set down a golf ball and drove it into a kid's ass thirty feet away. The kid yelled, and then another ball was in flight, skipping off the walls and down the hall. They hid out in their rooms cursing him and cheering him on, ducking in and out as each ball took flight.

When he was out of golf balls, he went back into his room and lay down again. They were back in the hall, saying his name, whispering it, yelling it. When next they saw him, he was standing outside his door with Henry's sixteen-pound Personal 300 Urethane bowling ball.

Redfield reared back and let it go, sending it rolling down the hall. *Thunk, rum, rum, rum, rum, rum, rum, rum . . . wham,* right into the resident adviser's door, tearing out the hinges, busting the lockset into little pieces and spraying them in the air. Archie, the R.A., came staggering out, ashen and drunk.

"Goddamnit, Redfield. Now look what you've gone and done."

They looked at each other from the length of the hall. First Archie started to laugh and then Redfield laughed, while the others watched from their rooms wondering what was so funny.

An hour later the dean showed up. He knocked quietly on Redfield's door, then let himself in. He sat down on Henry's bed and lit a cigarette.

"What's the story, Ray?"

"Real good. I'm doing fine," Redfield said, splashing some Johnnie Walker into a tumbler. He thought the dean said, How are you doing, Ray. Those are the kinds of things he isn't good with.

"I called your father, Ray, when you wouldn't answer my notes."

"You called my father Ray?"

The dean and Redfield's father went to college together. They had the kind of friendship you were supposed to make in college, the kind where you can call somebody and ask a favor. Redfield was a favor.

"You stopped going to classes," the dean said. "I wanted to see what the story was. Your father wouldn't talk to me. Your mother said he'd be in communication. I was a little saddened by it all. Now there's this bowling ball incident."

"My father's name isn't Ray."

"He sent me this postcard."

The dean handed a postcard to Redfield. It was of a dog hung by the neck and there was an Asian man standing off to its right, boulders and trees in the background. On the back it said, *Picnic of Death, South Korean dog hanged . . . then eaten.* There were also words in his father's hand. They said, *Cut it off and kill it.*

"I called your mother again and she said for you to travel a little bit. She said maybe you needed a little vacation. Is that what you want, Ray?"

"Yeah. I guess so."

The dean told him good luck, he told him he liked him and the door would be open when he wanted to come back to college, reminded him of how much it meant to his father.

He didn't know he was scaring Redfield. Redfield wanted the door closed, some door, any door. He hadn't spoken to his father since he left in September, and what had been said was said in anger.

He thought, If I don't know what I can do, I want to know what I can't do. If I don't know what's ahead, I'll settle for knowing what isn't behind. I *want* to burn a few bridges. Can't you see you're killing me? What he really wanted to do was go home, but home was the farm in Conquest and he didn't known if it was there.

His father was planning on selling the farm. It was property he'd bought as an investment, but Redfield had moved in while he was still in high school and started working the land. There was an eight-room farmhouse on ninety acres that rested gently to the north bank of the Seneca River. Redfield raised heifers and grew alfalfa and planted Christmas trees. When his father told him he needed to go to college, Redfield said he'd rather not. That's when his father told him he had to because he was selling the farm.

"Where's Henry tonight?"

"Probably fell asleep in the library."

The dean looked at the stack of books on Redfield's side of the room: *The Kama Sutra of Vatsyayana; Butch Cassidy: My Brother; Studies of Savages and Sex; The Decorated Body; Jewish Folklore; Terrible Kisses; Eat Not This Flesh: Food Avoidances in the Old World.*

"Good luck, Ray," he said again, and left.

Redfield hooked a bottle of Henry's Ritalin and made for I-81, pulling rpm's to be gone and to be quick about it. He wanted whole distance between where he was and where he'd be.

Settling down into the engine, wheeling down the road, he clutched big worries he'd done something wrong he couldn't remember. Maybe he was really going north, not south. He watched the roadside and was relieved whenever he saw the sign I-81 SOUTH. But going the wrong way was a feeling he could never shake.

I-81 wasn't far from his home. It was like a long driveway he was on, only he was going in the opposite direction. He was going south on the Confederate Highway, piloting along the spine of Virginia by now.

He went inside himself to find a place to be while he drove the long dark miles making hours disappear, having no recollection of living them. He found other stuff to think about, the blue vein on the white breast of a woman he knew and wouldn't mind knowing again sometime. His mother, his lovers, his cousin. He'd disappointed his father and disappointed the dean. He felt guilt and thought how easy that could turn to hate if some love didn't intervene, but what kind of love?

There was a girl he knew at college. They were close for some days in the fall. He'd tried to see her a few hours ago to say he was leaving to travel a little bit, but she wouldn't let him in. Thinking about her, he was to the point of almost crying when he hit a dip in the road and his big ribs screamed with glowing pain. He learned to think a little less. At least for a while.

*

At night the troopers go home. That was when he made his best time. That was when the incinerators turned on. Smokestacks blew and river valves went open on corroded pipes. The night dumpers wandered the back dirt roads.

Next rest stop twenty-one miles. He thought, There is no rest for the wicked. Something his mother would tell him and smile as she said it, like it was good news.

Will I ever play this back? Will there ever be a rerun? Will I ever be around to see it? Am I just young and filled with fancy thoughts about my own death? What's so bad about that? I have had an awfully good time.

Bingo. A hundred miles gone. Twenty more of those and that's how far I'll be from home.

Virginia, early in the morning, somewhere around Wytheville. He'd been driving all night. Know how it is. A descent into the greasy South, land of yellow eyeballs. Time goes that way when you're on the road. Time. Gravity bends both time and space. Without an event, there is no time. Time is on no one's side.

The big front windows of all the world's 7-Elevens, AM-PMs, Mini Marts. He stood at the pump and looked inside like it was a TV and there was a family or two, groceries on the shelves like in a pantry. Tables and chairs. Someone's kitchen with the doors off the cupboards. You all come in. The big substations of America. The big eastern rivers, Potomac, Susquehanna, Hudson, Connecticut. Church bells. Was it Sunday again so soon?

He stepped inside the convenience store and he was in the world where people talked and it was loud and their mouths were huge and out of synch with the words. The faces, the perfume, her hair, her eyeshadow, the way her body seemed to pulse. The truck driver's hair standing on end. The tattoos embroidered on his arm. The way they seemed raised and throbbing. Fluorescent light.

He couldn't wait to get outside, alone in the dark, but it was now close to daylight.

Bluefield, he read. I am Redfield. In Bluefield.

The sun came up in Tennessee that first morning. It was cold and he yawned. He stretched on the bike, arching and rolling his back, enduring the pain. The lights were still on and the road went white. It was hard to see, and it would be some time before his eyes adjusted.

Outside Bristol he took a concrete drainage ditch down to a creek that shot under the highway. He descended the concrete path into a pocket of mist. He hoped there was a way to turn around at the bottom or that the creek was shallow enough to ford. Anyways, it'd make a nice home if you were a copperhead. This was where he slumped back and started shutting down his body and then he was asleep, dreaming about women, dreaming he was still riding.

He was soon in one of his waitress riffs. He was sitting at the Woolworth's lunch counter filling out magazine subscription cards. He gave them to the waitress, asked her to mail them. She took them from his hand. It was an act of faith. He ordered the rice pudding and she brought it to him. He liked the idea of ordering rice pudding in Woolworth's.

After an hour he stirred. He couldn't figure out where he was. He couldn't remember sleeping. So silent. So dark. His head so heavy. And then he realized he still had his helmet on.

He got it off and washed his face in the creek. He walked the cattails. The ground was dry and the path up was a straight shot. He started the bike, busted through the cattails and rode to the interstate. There was a Tennessee state trooper waiting for him at the top.

Redfield hit the kill switch and dodged up the banking,

then let the machine coast back down. The trooper's name bar said DUPREE.

"License and registration."

Redfield handed them over, along with his college ID and fishing license. Dupree started to laugh.

"What the fuck's wrong with you," Redfield said.

"Raymond Romeo Redfield. What kind of name is that?"

"My name."

"I guess, but it's kind of like a boy named Sue. Sorry I laughed. That Johnny Cash kills me."

"It's an old family name," Redfield said. "What's your name?"

"Johnny. Johnny Dupree."

"What the hell kind of name is Johnny Johnny for a guy your age. Little old for highway patrol aren't you?"

"Listen, son, adolescence can be a fatal disorder."

"I've always found life to be that way."

Johnny Dupree pushed his hat back on his head and massaged his brow. He looked at the registration. Looked again at the license.

"That sure is a beautiful bike. Is it the new model?"

"Yes," Redfield said. "I picked it up at the factory in York a few weeks ago."

"I used to ride one, but then they put me in a car. I miss it. Where you headed?"

"West."

"Watch the speed and watch where you bed down. Okay?"

"Yeah," Redfield said, softening. He liked Johnny Dupree. He could see how he'd gotten to be old and didn't really know how.

"Sorry about the name. It is kind of odd. I've never seen it before and I thought I'd seen them all."

"When my mother and her sister were in high school, they played Romeo and Juliet. They had to wrap bandages around their chests. Like Judy Garland in *The Wizard of Oz.*"

"Dorothy."

"Yeah, Dorothy."

"Well, have a good 'un," Johnny Dupree said, tipping his hat.

"You too."

Johnny Dupree stood at the guardrail, watching as Redfield disappeared down the road, the green juniper tall and plump on the road banks and median. File upon file of juniper. There were horses in the meadows, sorrels, and chestnuts with long tails and swept manes, their heads cocked, their noses to the wind. They were beautiful animals, Johnny Dupree thought. They certainly were.

*

Playing tag through the mountains with the big rigs. Redfield was on the road remembering geometry class, Xeno's paradox. He could always figure to be halfway there, and if he kept doing that he'd never really get there, never eclipse the space between him and the rear end of an eighteen-wheeler.

There was the smell of brakes burning, the way it

lingered on the long hills. The sheer aluminum backs of trailer trucks flexing in the sunlight.

Automobiles. The driver in front of him kept looking down into his lap. Maybe he was getting a blow job. Maybe he'd gone numb and had to check to see if it was still happening. Redfield passed on the pegs and looked in. Nothing. The bike sputtered and he had to go on reserve. He hated getting gas because he had to pass the same people all over again.

Knoxville smelled like spray paint.

He passed a long black Cadillac and looked to see if Hank Williams's ghost was riding in the backseat, but he wasn't. Not today.

Up the road there was a gathering. Gold Wings. Swarms of them on the road. They were going east and west. They'd filled the rest stops. They all waved to him and had little toys attached to their bikes that waved too. He thought, Clouds of mystery surround the ignorant and the brilliant. Tell it.

He crossed Chaney Ford River and an exit for Juliet Road outside Nashville. That made him smile. Then there was Nashville Electric Service, a big squat round stone building, a fortress of power. Redfield tucked his head and kept pushing.

West, west, west was Memphis and that was where he'd spend the night.

He came to a detour and the road narrowed to one lane. He stopped behind the car in front of him. It was a slow black El Dorado that passed him some miles back on the right, the blinker on for ten miles. What can you say about someone who drives down the highway with their blinker on and doesn't know it? He waited for ten minutes as traffic stopped and cars stacked up behind him. He couldn't take the wait any longer, so he swung onto the strip of blacktop between the car and the concrete barrier. He pulled up alongside the driver and told him his blinker was on.

"I know," the guy said.

"Well, what the fuck are you doing driving around giving off a stupid false signal like that?"

"It's broken."

"Oh."

Redfield let out the clutch and motored along the shoulder, passing as many as a hundred cars. One driver pulled out to cut him off, resentful of his mobility. Redfield swooped behind and passed him on the right, kicking his door as he went by. Another mile and he saw what was holding traffic. There was a construction crane lying in the road with a man under it. The man had an immense tongue. Other men stood around, helpless, waiting for something strong enough to lift the boom.

Redfield squeezed past, pulled off the road and went thumping cross-country for a quarter mile until the road opened up. He wanted to get as far away from there as he could.

Is your headache gone?"

It's evening in New Mexico. He's just getting up from another long sleep. Having him here in the house is a comfort. She thinks maybe she won't tell him about the baby. She just won't say anything. She asks him again about his headache.

"Yes. I kind of miss it," he says.

He sits at the table and holds his head in his hands.

"So what happened?" she says.

"I think I'm going blind."

"Redfield, why?"

"Well not right now, but when I get really old. Maybe when I die."

"Fuck you."

He sips at his coffee, looks to find her legs. They are so beautiful. She is so beautiful.

"I had a job working in a quarry," he says. "There aren't many jobs left that can kill you, so I was lucky to get this one." He unfolds his knife and pares a thumbnail. "Did you know that in South Africa they used to collect ostrich eggs and black women would sit on them in shifts to hatch them?"

"Where'd you hear that?"

"Old Black Dog told me so."

"The ribs, Redfield."

He looks around the room, at the walls, at the ceiling, at the floor, at the white-draped furniture. His mind dodges. He thinks not to tell as a way of beginning a new life. Breathe, he tells himself, breathe.

"You always hear stories about danger," he says, fighting the drama in his voice. "It's like they're passing it on to you. Cables slip, chains break, stuff falls. The other guys, they wait around for the new guy to say or do something stupid. Like new guys bring their own star and until people know whether it's good or bad, they stay clear. One man dies for every seven stories. One man dies for every million spent. One man dies for every bridge. One man dies every day in the mines. Shit like that.

"The Department of Labor sends out Fatalgrams. They

go like: A sixty-eight-year-old man with forty-six years' mining experience was fatally injured when he jumped from the crane he was operating as it overtraveled the edge of an embankment. A laborer, age twenty, was electrocuted when he attempted to start a water transfer pump. A thirty-two-year-old miner with fifteen years' experience fatally injured when struck by a rock fall from above the portal of a new adit. Twenty-eight-year-old front-end-loader operator with ten years' mining experience fatally injured when another front-end loader backed over him. It's really quite romantic."

"What about you?"

"I was kind of like the last one. I was on the ground. We had to jump-start one of the rigs and I got pinched."

"My God, you could have been killed."

"My kidneys were traumatized. They gave me codeine. They said I'll be okay in a while or I won't. All the equipment's being moved out to Oklahoma, where it's lawless. They wanted me to disappear. They didn't want to get shut down before they could get out of Dodge."

"Redfield. You're telling me you went to the doctor?"

"No."

"Why not?"

"You know how a scalded cat runs?"

"Is that supposed to explain something?"

"Look. I don't know why I do what I do."

Juliet crosses her arms and shakes her head. She feels like crying but doesn't, and it makes her ache. She feels a little angry because he's brought these problems with him. She wanted him to be his old self, moody and young and strong and funny. Not injured.

"I'm healing," he tells her. "It may take some weeks."

"I thought you were supposed to be in college."

"I graduated."

"You don't graduate in a year."

"It was the Ritalin, what can I say. I took about fifty classes all at once. I was after some universals. My roommate has narcolepsy and his father is a doctor, so he's got some wicked stuff in his medicine bag and gives me a taste."

"You quit, didn't you. You know your father had his heart set on it. You have to go back."

"I know. The door is open. I still have library books I owe. You don't think they'd let me go with books due?"

"Didn't you like school?"

"I'm too old. I'm old, old, old."

She sits at the table across from him. She wants to say, It's all in a lifetime or When the going gets tough or something like that, but she knows he's heard it all before, and besides, she feels no conviction. She takes his hand in hers.

"You boys," she says.

"What?"

"You do that all the time. You hurt yourselves so women will love you."

"No we don't. No we don't."

"Yes you do. You punch a wall and break your hand

or you play football or you make a war so we'll feel sorry for you and love you. Women love wounded boys."

"Shhh," he says, his finger to his lips. "It really does hurt to talk."

He gets up and goes back to bed.

★

Late that night they both wake up happy. They ride down 66 in Albuquerque. Juliet loves the motorcycle. It's Cuban night at Fo-Fo's, so they eat ropa vieja and drink Red Spike beer. Next to their table is an artist who paints furniture. Redfield tells him how his old man passed through here in 1948, how he's reenacting the trip as one of those discovery things. The artist says 1948's when he graduated from high school in Sante Fe.

He says, "It was still a time of innocence. We'd drive around the square all night long singing 'Ninety-Nine Bottles of Beer' and go down to Juárez on the weekend and get drunk. The most pornographic thing I ever saw was a flip book with Popeye getting a hard-on. That was when Wheaties was still the breakfast of champions."

Later they follow the band to the El Rey Theatre. It's a Reggae Fest, featuring Quest with special guest Spiritual Healing.

Redfield thinks, Sometimes you can't avoid such stuff, and he holds her as they dance, his hands at her ribs. He squeezes and her breath comes out. He gets his mouth to her ear.

"I want to write a book called *Pilots on Drugs*. It'd be

like an old-time movie. A bad movie. But that's basically the concept."

"You're just talking."

"The only things I remember about the X ray was when the technician would move me. Her breasts touched me. They were like sleeping puppies. I thought she must touch a lot of men like that before she shoots the X ray through them. Maybe she likes it."

"Maybe she doesn't even notice."

They sit at a table off to the side. Redfield gets his back against the wall, where he can see all who pass by. He thinks how if someone comes in with an Uzi, he'll throw his body over Juliet's, letting the rounds take residence in his back.

"What ya doing, Redfield?"

"Thinking about getting me some leg."

She smiles, then puts her leg in his lap.

"Don't do that, Miss Juliet. I may be your cousin, but I am a man."

"Boy."

"Boy. Man. What the fuck."

★

Back at the house Juliet goes inside while Redfield smokes a joint the artist gave him.

He calls to her from the patio.

"Come out with me, Juliet. Come out tonight. Come out. Come out."

She comes to the door and hangs at the jamb. She tells

herself it's okay he's here. He's noisy. He's big. Has
gravity.

"I have to stay out of the night," she says. "It's come
to do things to me. I don't know why I'm here. I don't
know why I'm talking to you. I don't know why I do
what I do. Is it too much to want to know? I think I
drank too much beer."

From where they are, they can see Sandia Crest, a wall
of granite rising in relief five thousand feet from the
desert floor, its ascent an abrupt and rugged wall. It floats
in the night sky, a presence they don't talk about.

"I travel at night," he says. "I prefer it. I like to see
the country in the dark. I like the way the light slides
along the chrome. It's smooth and even. When it's first
morning sometimes you can shut down the lights and
drive by the moon. When I travel through your town,
think of me while you sleep in your bed."

"You talk a lot. Is it only talk?"

"Romeo and Juliet. They were cross-eyed lovers."

"Star-crossed."

"Jesus. Didn't you read the book? We're going to die
because the mail doesn't get through. I don't want to do
that. I don't want my life depending on the U.S. Postal
Service. They've raised the rates, you know. It's a way of
breaking down communication. They don't want us
writing to each other. Revolution."

"You sound like your father with all his conspiracy
theories. I'm going to bed. I'm still a little drunk."

He goes to where she is and blows a lungful of smoke
into her mouth.

He reaches inside the neck of her blouse and holds her breast, his thumb on her nipple, and then he kisses her.

"I rode twenty-seven-hundred miles thinking about doing that."

"I've been waiting," she says. "I've been waiting all my life wondering if it'd ever happen, but I didn't expect it."

"I'm sorry. I couldn't help myself. What's that perfume?"

"Emeraude."

"Jesus. It's kind of delightful, isn't it? Smells like some anatomies I've known. I go crazy."

"Don't be disgusting."

"I was thinking of wet horses. Your horse, as a matter of fact."

She takes him inside and leads him down the hall. He sits on her bed, his feet holding to the floor. He bends down and collects a few days' worth of her underclothes that are strewn on the tiles. He holds them to his face, breathes their scent deep into his head. All that cotton and nylon and satin and lace blended with the smell of her body.

"I know a secret," she says.

"What?"

"You used to dress up in my underwear when you were a little boy."

"I have to tell you it'd make me hard to feel that material, but then I wouldn't know what to do with it."

"You're so silly. You'd hang my dolls, too."

"And for that I've always been sorry. The poor little

dickens. That kind of makes me candidate for serial murderhood.''

"There are crossroads in all our lives."

He laughs and she does too, but they wonder if they're laughing over different stuff. He gets up and leaves the room. He's begun to sweat and can't stop himself. The pot has brought on his appetite and it's something he now feels raging inside him, but thinking about the act of eating makes him sick to his stomach.

Outside, the swamp cooler goes to hum, blowing air through a drum of wet pads, blowing it into the house to answer the heat.

Juliet is happy for those small favors of memory, her life before she gave birth. Maybe she can patch it together that way.

She calls from her bedroom down the hall, "Come back in here and talk to me. Bring me a beer from the fridge."

I am sweating, he thinks. He feels the salty waters of his body slide down his spine. He goes in and stands beside her bed. She is wearing only her panties and has nice breasts for a cousin.

She sings: *Do you know the muffin man, the muffin man, the muffin man? Do you know the muffin man who lives on Drury Lane?*

She sings it like it's the blues. He's not even sure it's the truth she's singing that way, but that's how it comes into his head. In the light of the darkness her white skin makes this look like a negative. Sometimes we are close, he thinks. Sometimes we are not. He sits down on her bed again. He has presents for her. He should go get them from his pack. He gives her the beer. Her hair really is white.

"Look at us," she says. "This sucks."

Redfield doesn't say anything. She touches his head with her foot and says his name. She strokes his cheek with her toes and feels how wet his face is.

"Redfield. Honey?"

She sets the beer on the floor and gets on her knees, her hands on his back. She can see he's crying.

"What's the matter?"

"I have to pee," he says.

"I'll help," she whispers.

Out in the night she holds him in her hand, her face between his shoulder blades. They're standing on the edge of the bosque, the cottonwood forest along the banks of the Rio Grande. She starts to laugh.

"What's so funny?"

"I remember when you used to have such a little baby dick. In the summers I'd sit for you. I'd have to change your diaper and you had such a cute little penis."

"You walk like a cow," he says. "You don't look like one, but you walk like one."

"Aren't you sweet."

"It's the way your legs go first and then your body follows. You know what I mean. It's sort of elegant."

A sound comes from the bank of the irrigation ditch.

"Listen!" she says.

"What?"

"The weeper," she whispers. "La Llorna. She's been wailing at night for two hundred years."

"Who is she," Redfield says, determining not to believe.

"She's a widowed mother who drowned her children so she'd be free to marry another man, but he rejected her. She dresses in black and wears chains. When she lets out a wail there will be a death in the family."

"Do you hear her?"

"No, but for a second I thought I did."

When they go inside she peels off his T-shirt and unwraps his ribs. He tells her he won't let La Llorna get her and she believes him.

"Did you leave anything behind," she whispers.

She says it in a way so it's not a question but a wish he didn't. He tells her the battlefields are still there, Gettysburg, Shiloh, Antietam.

"We shouldn't be sleeping together," he says. "I'll go in the other room. It isn't funny anymore."

"I don't care," she says, "but it was you. You felt me up. You've never done that before."

"I had to touch another human being. A woman."

"I'm not a woman. I'm your cousin."

"Same difference."

She looks at him. He doesn't speak again.

"You know," she says, "that's the first time that saying ever made much sense to me. Same difference. There is something I have to tell you."

But it's late and they're tired. They fall to sleep, Redfield to dream about a waitress in Memphis.

Juliet to dream she's still waiting for him. She's back in that time when she was alone and was thinking she'd already killed herself.

6

As the story gets told, east of Memphis was a great intersection of power lines, the Wolf River, pine forests, the Hatchie River.

Redfield started at the river bluffs and worked his way east seven blocks. Beale Street, Memphis, Tennessee. Elvis. B. B. King. Isaac Hayes. Al Green. Jerry Lee Lewis. Charlie Rich. Old Mr. Haney.

Guys playing guitars under the trees in the park. Elvis is a pink Cadillac. A Stutz Bearcat. Sixteen-carat diamond T.C.B. ring. Taking care of business. He liked his girls young, in white panties. Couldn't have been all that bad. The Lisa Marie and Jet Star Planes.

Redfield stayed at a Days Inn. Shower and bed. The windows of the other rooms were papered with Elvis sacred rummage—posters, T-shirts, toys, Elvis toys.

Redfield going to Graceland.

"I want to see Elvis," he said politely to the guide. "I thought you kept him in a glass coffin like the Russians do John Lennon."

The guide didn't stop telling the tour group about Elvis finery and largess, dining room, TV room, gold piano, pool room, cloth room, plywood in the hall, jungle room. People were crying. The young punk couple, the German design student, the honeymooners, the old Brits.

Vernon's office, pool, racquetball court, guns, badges, movie posters, gold records, keys to the cities of America. Let me in. Let me in.

"Where's the King's stash? I want to see his medicine cabinet." Redfield worried he was being a pest, but these were some things he wanted to see.

Elvis's fourteen-ton tour bus: a 1959 flexible VL 100 coach powered by a turbo Cummins diesel engine with 140-gallon fuel tank. The floor is lead-lined, to keep motor and road noise to a minimum. Swivel recliner easy chair and a double bed. Electric range, rotisserie, oven, refrigerator, garbage disposal and trash compactor. Full shower, marine commode, vanity, medicine cabinet, gold-plated fixtures. Cards and Yahtzee. Eight-tracks. Joking. Singing. Eating. Sleeping. Viva. Viva.

Elvis is: teddy bears, albums, clocks, valentines, Brazil, snapshots, postcards, mugs, glasses, T-shirts, videos.

Three generations of loving Elvis. From Memphis to the promised land. Goodbye to Elvis.

Redfield turned to the German design student.

"That sumbitch in two years gobbled nineteen thousand doses of narcotics, stimulants, sedatives and antidepressants. When he died he had in his body codeine, morphine, Quaalude, Valium, Valmid, Placidyl, Amytal, Nembutal, Carbrital, Demerol, Elavil, Aventyl and Sinutab. Sinutab, can you believe it? If that all don't make him the King, nothing does."

Elvis security came to escort Redfield outside the wrought-iron gate, outside the grounds of Graceland.

He stood on the sidewalk yelling for them to *set Elvis free, set Elvis free.*

The blood surged in his body and his temples throbbed. He felt something go in one of his eyes. It was a blood vessel. He'd done it before. He had a flashback to earlier in the day, the guy under the crane. He realized the enormous tongue was the guy's intestines, and his guts began to lurch against his bruised ribs. He went down on his hands and knees in daylight in Memphis and wretched streams of bitter fluid on the sidewalk.

When he could walk again, he went back to the motel and got inside where there was no light. He stretched out on his bed and it rolled like the ocean. The ceiling pirouetted like cloud movies. He kept being afraid he'd go into orbit.

When it was dark and he was tired, he was calm enough to go out again. He went to Tiffany's and G. G.'s

Angels down on Winchester, the finest in adult entertainment, where the experiences never end. Some of the girls were pretty; some weren't. Some were beautiful and made your sacred heart melt. He didn't find what he was looking for, so he left for the blues houses and pawnshops.

He watched the junkies cross Beale on the diagonal. They were easy to spot. They comported themselves most sanely, like businessmen or ministers. He followed them into the alley, where they burned piles of charcoal briquettes, not so much because the night was cool but because the day had been so hot and their blood ran thin.

He wondered how safe it was out here on the side streets and in the alleys off Beale, but then he realized he was the kind of person most people were afraid of, at least the people he was with now. They fingered buttons, talked fast and heard voices. Redfield smoked deeply, deep hits. He had light bulbs behind his eyes. He was dying. He sang . . . living on the road my friend, gonna keep you free and clean. Now you wear your skin like iron, breath as hard as kerosene. Weren't your mama's only boy, but her favorite one it seems. She began to cry when you said goodbye and sank into your dreams . . .

On the way back to the motel, Redfield pulled into a Bob's Big Boy.

He ordered coffee and Coke and orange juice. Then he put his head down on the counter and closed his eyes. The waitress let him keep it there awhile because the night was slow, and besides, his head rested neatly on the menu like he was way farsighted. Finally she went over to him, afraid he'd spill his drinks, afraid maybe he couldn't see or read.

"Hey," she said. "Who are you? We think you're a movie star. There's something about you."

"I'm an actor," he said, rubbing his eyes. "I'm researching the role of my life. So I can make a movie of it. It's something we're all doing. The noise in here is immense."

"You're researching your life?"

"Yes. I've done this all before only I didn't know it at the time because I was just genetic material."

"She thinks you're Tom Cruise. You're not Tom Cruise, are you?"

The waitress looked over to her friend at the other end of the counter, then back to Redfield.

"No, I'm not," he was saying. "At least not anymore, but then again he isn't, either. We used to be, but we're not anymore."

"It's Tom Cruise," she yelled to her friend. "I knew it was."

"Ask him how he got the scar on his face," her friend yelled back.

"I was cut and when they stitched me up it left a scar. What scar are you talking about, anyways?"

"He isn't Tom Cruise," her friend yelled from her end of the counter.

"Not anymore. He used to be. He's changing his image. Will you do a scene with us in it or people like us?"

"Of course."

"Who will play us?"

"You can play yourself or someone else can."

She had her hands on the counter. Redfield looked down at them. The skin was so white it was almost translucent, veinless. It was tan-dusted and her touch on the Formica seemed like air, so soft he had to look away.

"They're my best feature," she said. "I hoped you'd notice them. I want to become a hand model when I finish high school."

She touched his hand and he had to look where she was touching him to know she was.

"So what time do you get off?"

"I don't get off."

"Come on. What time do you get off?"

"I get off every time my boyfriend gets me off."

"Oh, I get it. Why don't you get off with me?"

"I won't do that, but I'll talk to you."

Redfield laughed, thinking how heavy her breasts must be inside her smock. The other waitress came over. She was older and had been around, had that I-used-to-talk-to-assholes-like-you-too way about her. Redfield could see now she was a waitress too, wondered how he had missed that fact and felt spooked.

She said, "What do you think of women who wear glasses?"

"I don't much care as long as they got a fat butt. Wanna see me blow milk out my nose?"

"Look, honey, one piece of white trash to another, why don't you get your helmet off my fucking counter?"

"Are you eating something or do you always sound like that? You ought to stuff your mouth with stones and go yell at the ocean. Did a guy named Old Black Dog stop here and ask for me?"

★

It was late when Redfield got back to the motel. He went through the pains of undressing. He risked lying down on the bed, risked the surges and tweaks in his body. They came quickly and for some time, then dissipated. He thought he might even sleep a little, and then the young waitress came knocking. She told him she'd decided to take a chance. She told him all the men she knew thought they were Elvis or Richard Petty or Lionel Richie.

"That's the men," he said. "What about the women?"

"Well, the women are in love with the men."

"Come in," he told her. "Make yourself comfy."

"My mother used to work at Woolworth's," she said, sitting cross-legged on the bed and knitting her perfect fingers together. "When things got slow she'd let the monkeys out to run around. She has these long fingernails and she paints them and every time she scratches herself it's like it's my own skin. Can I ask you a question?"

"Sure."

"Are you a doctor? We used to have a doctor around here who rode a motorcycle."

"No. I'm not a doctor."

"Can I tell you something?"

"Sure."

"My mother taught her German shepherd to sniff crotches so as to embarrass people."

"That's a funny thing to do."

"Know how she did it? She slathered her own with gravy and let the dog lick it up."

"Jesus Christ," Redfield said.

"Can I ask you something?"

"What?"

"Are we gonna nurge or sit here and talk all night?"

Redfield remembered the tongue again and it was like he'd busted through ice, only it was the sky and he was falling forever. It was the only memory he never wanted to have again and here it was. It raged in his head, vandalized his mind. His stomach began to roll. He made the bathroom just in time to puke water and Coke and orange juice and coffee into the toilet, his guts heaving at his ribs like men with hammers.

When he came out, she was gone.

★

In the morning he rode into Memphis for coffee and a newspaper. In the paper were symbols: a lion, a lizard and a camel. There was a heavy-lidded eye over each and they were all of two inches by two inches. He thought they spoke to him, but first he had to know they weren't something civic, weren't something the chamber of commerce spawned.

He asked a cop and a waitress. He asked the guy who

sold him the paper. He asked a hot dog vendor. He walked the streets that smelled like piss. Nobody knew. He asked some Japanese tourists, but he was not sure what they knew because they didn't speak English. They only smiled at him as if it were a reasonable defense against maniacs. He watched a four-foot homeless woman wearing a cast-off Laura Ashley walk up the block. She was bent double and needed to crank her head sideways to see where she was going and walk sideways to get there. It took about a month. He wandered into Confederate Park, strolled amongst the winos sleeping on the benches or gazing out over the Mississippi, seeing something way off in Arkansas.

He read a sign, FREESTONE PEACHES. He said to no one, "If I were from Memphis, I'd sing the blues too."

He dropped his right shoulder into the ramp, pounded his tires up the asphalt, passed the substation, passed the pyramid and slid off across the Mississippi River in the direction of Little Rock. He thought, My life in shorthand. He thought, 1954, Little Rock. The 82nd Airborne. Death from the sky.

*

On down the road it was a hot muzzle of air that enveloped him. He could hear the sound of tires peeling off the hot sucking tar. Route 40 West and West and West. New army jeeps that looked like turtles came his way. Eisenhower built these highways for days like today, days of mobilization. Was there another war and nobody'd told him?

Up ahead someone must've broken open the road because there was the smell of old shoes in the gray belt of haze.

Cache River. White River. He drank Mountain Valley Spring Water: the choice of Elvis, bottled at its natural spring source in Hot Springs National Park, Arkansas. There was a dead armadillo.

Around Lonoke, the air got even heavier, running with its own sweat. Kind of cool. The cars started coming with their lights on. He was afraid it was going to rain. Thus far he'd been blessed by the weather god.

He got done thinking this and the rain came in a blast for a quarter mile, hot rain, hissing on the tar. Ahead was an overpass, but the road turned dry so he kept moving. In this after-rain world, the air smelled like chlorine, like riverbeds. In a few miles he was dry.

A car passed outside Little Rock. A girl with bare shoulders was driving. She was blond and had her hair tied back. She was an American girl, with her boyfriend asleep on the seat beside her. Redfield passed her and she didn't look his way.

Redfield sings: I see my light come shining, from the west down to the east, any day now, any day now, I shall be released.

He wondered why the light came from the west to the east. Is it because it's evening and the sun has passed over the songwriter? Is there something about a light from the west? Is it just to make the friggin' rhyme?

He tucked in behind a Kenworth gunning for the west to see this light. He rode in the draft, the hands of truck-made wind pushing him along. A slip in concentration and at any moment he could be plastered against the truck's rear end. He thought, This is my life too. He thought it like a question.

He was passing through time zones, leaving the hours behind, gaining on life. If he could go fast enough he'd run with the light. It'd never get dark. He'd get younger, be a child, be unborn. Alone. Back in time. Or was it the other way around and he was expending his life, getting older. He began to panic. At seventy miles an hour, twelve feet behind eighteen wheels of driving steel with the wind at your back, well, this was not a good thing to do.

He came across a double-wide, tipped over and splayed open beside the highway. He went past, then stopped and turned around. The guy was okay. He was sitting there beside the road smoking a cigarette.

"Has somebody gone for help?" Redfield said. He said it as if it were for him. He said it like, Boy am I glad to see you.

"Yeah, a guy just left out of here."

"You dropped their house."

"Yeah. I dropped their fucking house."

"Whose house is it? Do they know you dropped it?"

"I don't know."

"I wonder if they know."

"I highly doubt it. It just happened."

"That's the way it goes sometimes."

"Yeah," the guy said, brightening up. "Sometimes that's the way it goes. It's kind of like a broken home."

★

Redfield created a rise and saw sun over water. It could have been the ocean. It was huge in his mind and went on forever and then he was in the middle of it on the road. The air smelled like deep water, clean and fresh. The water was dusty blue and marbled with light. People were skiing.

There was a car in the left-hand lane and it wouldn't get over. In the passenger seat there was a woman with her foot on the dash. He thought how beautiful she was. Ahead was a guy with a skinny neck and a bumper sticker that said PARTY NAKED.

"Shit," Redfield said. He was now far from home, out here in Oklahoma land. Somewhere around two thousand miles out, he figured, and it was like a long cord that was stretching and stretching. The further he got the more taut it became and he was waiting for it to snap. He looked at his watch and it was 3:50. He looked again and it was 4:50. He looked again and it was 5:50. He stopped for gas, saved his cash and traded the watch for a tank of unleaded.

He pulled into a rest stop down the road. On the door to the men's room was a sign.

Help. Man and wife are in need of help. We had truck trouble and it took what money we had for repairs. We are in need of gas and food. We are trying to get home to Lawton, Oklahoma. Any help will be appreciated. We are in the black GMC pickup truck with the camper on it. Thank you very much.

When Redfield came out, he gave them a ten-spot. The

guy had a big gut and carried himself as one with a
hidden disability. In the back of the pickup were blue tick
mattresses and furniture not worth hauling, but it was
theirs.

"Thank you," the wife said. "Very much appreciate it.
Every little bit helps."

Redfield didn't say anything. He gave off a tight smile
and got back on the road.

It was full dark by Oklahoma City and his eyes hadn't
adjusted fast enough and the lights sparkled and weaved
before him. The road went down and it looked as if it
was disappearing into a concrete barrier that turned out
to be a bridge crossing over top. He panicked for a
moment, afraid he'd taken a wrong turn and gotten
himself someplace dangerous. It smartened him up.

He saw where he was. There was more traffic now. He
kept seeing a billboard, a woman in a white bikini selling
Coors beer. He saw her again and again. He wanted her
to go away.

I don't want to be here, he thought. Why have I come
here against my will? I wish there were somebody waiting for me at home. Somebody I can think about a little
bit. Somebody I can miss and who will miss only me.

He tried to remember the name of Priscilla Presley's
favorite perfume, but he couldn't. It was on a sign in the
front of the tour bus and bottles of it were in the gift
shops, but he couldn't remember.

The traffic thinned and he felt better alone on the road.
He wished he could sing the blues like Roosevelt Booba

Barnes and then he went off in his head for some hours to eclipse the miles before him, to short out the substations, all lit and humming with electricity, to sniff the gas fields and their geysers of flame.

Off in his head, he solved extraordinary problems of mathematics, science, medicine, the humanities. He wrote poetry, saw music. The air filled with the smell of oil. The light from the stars in the sky. Howlin' Wolf in his head. To the right and left the earth was inky black, and he imagined it to be great seas of oil. And the distant light above. And this road is a causeway. People have told him, with your IQ you should be a genius. I was a genius and have long since abused myself into a state of average and like it better that way. Now there comes a momentary clearing, a moment of satorial splendor, and then it goes oblique. It fades away like blown dust.

The great lands west of Little Rock. Land stitched by the Canadian River, the Arkansas, the Cimarron and the Red River. The kind of land where you could start your own country and only need buy real estate from two or three people.

From the interstate he could see a man in his garage. He had a trouble light hanging from the hood of his pickup. Redfield couldn't hear anything, but saw him moving. The inside walls were plywood and hung with tools. Maybe he was waiting for his wife to get home. He was puttering at a workbench and by then Redfield was gone a half mile down the road.

A possum belly rattled by and Redfield went drunk on

the smell of cowshit wafting from the trailer. It must be
'round midnight. His odometer was just turning 666
again. He laughed. He knew there was a law of inci-
dence. He wondered what west Oklahoma looked like in
the daylight. The lit up signs were Anywhere, America.

West of Oklahoma, in the nation of Texas, he got high
on the smell of grain that now came with the cowshit.
Big silos showed in the night. To live here would be a
frightening thing. The thought of going outside to take a
leak and seeing the sky come down to the earth, to see
so many miles in all directions. It'd be like pissing in
public, even on the darkest night. To cross the threshold
of your door and enter the night would be to lose all
sense of space. You'd have to duck and walk with your
head down, cowed by the size of the sky, the smallness
of yourself.

He pulled in for gas and coffee. The tank full, he
staggered through the door and spilled coffee into Styrofoam. He tore open the whitener and dumped it into his
cup. He tore open another and this time dumped it into
the wastebasket.

"You look beat, son."

"I left Memphis this morning."

"You live over there near that Dollywood?"

"No. I live in upstate New York," he said, the lights
swarming like bees.

"Wouldn't ever want to go there. Better watch out for
the troopers. They'll have you back here for a money
order."

"They out tonight?"

"They're out every night. They already brought one fellow back here. He was from Connecticut. They won't let you out-of-staters go without paying the fine."

He could see the blinking lights of transmission towers. They were like stars that'd gone hot and burned holes in the sky. Tiny flames like pilot lights in gas ovens. The fronts of trucks looked pretty good right now. Too bad they were on the east highway.

This darkness in Texas. Redfield and the trucks. Their draft licking at his back. Their lights like embers in front of him: four, five, six, red, yellow, blue. They talked to each other with light. Flashing and blinking words. They said, You've cleared, time to cut in. They said, I'm coming. They said, Thank you.

They congregated in the rest areas, lined up like elephants, parked and dormant, engines idling, thrumming quietly, lights at rest. Dreams of women. Dreams of men. Dreams of horses. A graveyard of sorts.

The sky was soft coal black. He rode into the maw of another storm, praying he wouldn't get wet. It started to rain, drops like stones on the shell of his helmet. He pulled off the road and scuttled up under a bridge with his blanket.

Time passed. Dreams. Sometimes I hate my father because he told me how my life will be. He stole my life that way. He takes no pleasure in being right. He's sad about being right. He's sad about having a son who has made him tell the truth about life. Every time he looks at me, he sees what he used to be, sees what he was. It's all the more apparent to him what he's become. I think he's a great man, but he sees himself as having come to nothing. He says, I am truth, meaning me. He says to me, You are truth, rhymes with youth. It has to do with prospect and chance. I am irrefutable. I am undeniable. I am his flesh and blood. The only thing worse would be if I were a daughter, because daughters are a needle in the heart, while sons are only a hammer in the chest. My father loves me so much it leaves him weak. It's not the way he loves my mother. Loving her gives him joy. Makes him alive.

When he woke up he felt the burning in his guts and tried to doze off again, but someone was yelling to him, shining a light in his face. It was a state trooper standing on the road looking up at him.

"Buenos nachos," Redfield said.

"You can't be here."

"No lo contendere."

"Speak English?"

"Yeah."

"Get your smart ass down here."

Redfield came sliding down the concrete embankment, slowly, stiff-legged, remembering where he was.

"License and registration."

Redfield handed over his fishing license.

"Not this, wise guy."

"My mistake. I confused you with the game warden. I was thinking about going fishing in the morning."

"You ever been in any trouble?"

"Yeah, I used to wet the bed."

The trooper laughed at this. He knew who Redfield was.

"I was at a party and ate a goldfish once. I got sued and ended up on the *People's Court*. Judge Wapner found against me, but Rusty and Doug thought it quite comical. The wheels of justice just keep on turning and churning."

"You were on *People's Court*?"

"No. I made that up. I'm sorry to see how disappointed you are."

"I trust you are on your way out of the state."

"Yes I am, but you should only trust in God."

"Johnny Dupree said to say hello in case I saw you."

Redfield shook his head and started to laugh. His eyes watered and tears came.

"Where are you headed?"

Redfield dabbed at his cheeks. He was confused, trying to figure out whether he was laughing or crying and if he was crying, how come. He was taking in air, whole mouthfuls, he missed Johnny Dupree so much.

"I'm looking for a place to raise a family," he said.

"You have a family?"

"No. I figured I'd find a place to do it first."

★

Redfield pulled off the highway in Amarillo. He realized he'd been living on energy that just wasn't there. Sometimes you die.

At the Big Chain Hotel, the woman told him there was no room at the inn. No room in town. Seemed there was an air show this week.

"How 'bout if I lay down on that couch awhile?"

"No. I'm sorry," she said. This is the kind of thing they teach you to say in Big Chain Hotel school.

"There's a planter over there. I'll get in with the plants. I'll look like a plant."

"No. I'm sorry."

"Look. I'm from the national headquarters and have come to see how helpful you can be to weary, self-destructive travelers."

"No you're not."

"Okay, I'm homeless. I'm a statistic in the flesh. I really am. I'm a flatistic in the stesh."

"I'm sorry, there's nothing I can do."

"Being courteous is a start. Now look, you can take me into your home. It's a big house. You must have hundreds of rooms here."

"They're all taken."

"Well, put me up with somebody else like in *Moby Dick* or *Johnny Tremain*. Just knock on a door. Ask around. In all great literature people sleep in strange beds."

Redfield fought the urgency in his voice. He felt it to be unwrapping him.

"Sir, you will have to leave."

"*Sir,* that's good. Now hey, don't you want to be one of those thousand fucking points of light? At least let me give you my name so if I die tonight you can feel like shit."

"I don't want your name. Please go."

"I'll tell you anyways. My name is Raymond Romeo Redfield. RRR. Like 666, but my friends call me Horace. Actually, nobody calls me Horace. Horace is a guy I went to junior high with. One time we took a board and broke a window in a garage. He got the shaft. I got the lecture. It was on Einstein's theory of relativity. I didn't understand a goddamn word of it. Maybe relatives are a theory. You don't have any secret buttons down there, do you?"

"I'm going to call security."

"No. Wait. One more question?"

"What?"

"Is it true a dog's mouth is cleaner than a human's?"

She reached for the phone.

"You're supposed to say, A human's what? No, listen. Who pits all those olives? Did you know that in Germany they have words for things we already have perfectly good words for? I know every language but Greek. Sounds Greek to me. Here's one. How much wood could a woodchuck chuck if a woodchuck could chuck wood? What's up? The sky. My pants. What time is it? Time to hit the road."

Redfield went out the door into the warm night. He orchestrated his mouth with his arms. He thought about losing control, wondered if this is what it's like.

"Knock, knock," he yelled. "Who is it? I. P. Daily. Do you know the muffin man? Who puts the sound in Velcro? Is midnight twelve A.M. or twelve P.M.? How cold is a witch's tit? If Elvis Presley is dead, how come you never see him in the same place at once? Which is faster, the light of day or the dark of night? If a tree falls in the woods, does it make a sound? Who gives a shit?"

She came to the door and told him he was scaring her.

"Please don't let me go out there on the road. Lock me up in a closet. I think they botched my lobotomy. Say that ten times fast. How big do you think the rocks were in Little Rock?"

Redfield juked about the parking lot, kicking at bushes and clicking his heels, his whole body shivering with tongues of cold fire.

A car arrived. Young men in three-piece suits not much older than him. They stood at the glass doors watching him shimmy. He pointed up to the Big Chain Hotel sign. It welcomed lawyers and the bar association.

"Hey," he yelled to them. "What do you call three hundred lawyers at the bottom of the ocean?"

"A damn good start," they yelled back.

7

"I'm on a mission," he says in his sleep.

He's a boy, she thinks.

"Tough Jesus," he says.

Juliet sits on the edge of the bed filing her nails. She's been thinking about getting her life back together, collecting pieces that seem to be strewn across a continent. She'll hold off for a while. She's afraid it will be like finishing a jigsaw puzzle only to find some of it missing, never to be found. Silly thought. Silly puzzles. It's more like finishing the puzzle to find you're an amputee. What's the use. She'll file her nails. Maybe polish them.

She knows she'll forget what she's doing, end up with half a hand undone.

She remembers hearing her father say, There comes a time when all that's left to do is be happy for them or hurt for them. She starts to cry, lets the file go to the floor. When there are five fingers, what could half a hand be?

From far off comes a thunderhead dragging braids of rain. She goes into the bathroom and pulls up her T-shirt. Her navel looks like a lidded eye staring back at her. She used to think how it was such a pretty navel. Her breasts ache. She shuts off the light and expresses milk into the sink to relieve the pressure. When they are not so heavy, she touches water to her face, goes back into his bedroom and sits down.

I'm not so crazy right now, she thinks, then loses her breath to great wings in her stomach, a fist lodged in her throat.

"I am. I am," she cries. "I hurt. I hurt."

Redfield rolls around behind her. The whole bed moves when he does this. It undulates like land quakes, ocean waves. She's tired and queasy. She wants to step out of herself, not be who she is. If only she could stand up, get off that rocking bed. She pushes at her hair and tosses her head. She lies down and closes her eyes, wishes sleep into her life.

Redfield is dreaming a dream he's had before. He's in a coffee shop chatting up a pretty girl. It goes:

Tickle your ass with a feather?

Excuse me? she says.

I said, Particularly nasty weather.

No you didn't. You said, Tickle your ass with a feather.

I know. It's an old joke and I wanted to see if it worked in life.

It could, she says. This is Texas. I'm off in a half hour.

They go back to her condo and swim in the pool. In his dream, he thinks, this is nice because lately I've been dreaming about Texas.

I thought we'd do some Texas thing like swim in a creek or a stock tank. You know, chase out the water moccasins and the cottonmouths.

Well, I'm not from Texas. I'm from Florida.

Lightning begins to jag the sky and she puts her arms around him.

I'm nervous, she says. One time a thunderstorm set off my answering machine and my girlfriend told me it was a message from God.

She then turns into his mother and he says, Mommy, how does God get to Florida?

Redfield rolls to his back and moans. His ribs have come down on her shoulder. Reaching over, he grabs his wrist and drags his left arm onto his stomach. He breathes heavily, almost panting. He feels his body to be slick with sweat. He picks up his arm and raises it into the air, stretching it. She stirs in the bed beside him.

"What is it, hon?"

"You called me honey," he says between breaths.

"What is it? What's wrong?"

"It's my arm. It's gone dead on me."

"Your arm?"

"Yeah. When I sleep in a different bed, some nerve in my back gets pinched off."

"Do you want me to walk on your back?"

Redfield sits up and moans again. He goes light-headed and where he sits, the bed sinks. She can feel herself sliding into the depression. He rolls off the bed, intending to catch himself, but his left arm is limp. He lists toward the bed, bumping it a foot across the floor, then collapses, banging his head on the tiles.

"Oh," he says, and then starts to laugh, his chest thumping on the floor.

Juliet swings off the bed and steps onto his shoulders. She holds her arms out for balance while she shuffles up and down his spine. She concentrates on keeping balance. She is sure her life depends on it.

"I like that pain," he says, his voice muffled in the crook of his elbow. "The one in my shoulder and down the back of my arm. It's warm. I was playing football and went to tackle a guy and he ran right through my arm. It was like somebody let go a long, hot, thick elastic. They reached in, drew it out, pulled it to the max and then they let it go inside. *Sproing!* They did it again and it just kept going off. Over and over again. It was amazing. I love this hurt."

"The center of the back and the palms of the hands are the heart meridians," she says.

She peels off her T-shirt and throws it on the bed. Her breasts are swollen and wet. Now she's enjoying herself. She imagines this is what surfing must be like. She bends her knees a little and holds her arms out. She imagines she's under the big top and Redfield's an immense white horse with a chest that's four feet wide. He's cantering, his back lunging and rising in the rhythm of an easy gallop. She misses her horse.

"The days are getting shorter," she says. She can feel them. She didn't notice at first, but by now she knows it to be happening. She sees it and it's all she sees. The aloneness felt in the darkness of those close mountains. "You know," she says, "you look at satellite maps and this is the darkest state in the country. I have to go south. I get so morbid in the dark. I'm counting on you."

He tells her to stay high near his shoulders or low toward his ass. His ribs are like spikes under him. The pain is funny. It makes his eyes water.

"I like your cycle bike. I like riding it."

"Yes, I like riding too. Afterwards you've gotten somewhere, and getting there has left you tired and now you're out of harm's way. The broken white line. I love the way the light reflects on the toxic bogs down through the Oranges. All the land spangled with yellow and red lights. America the beautiful. I can see this all as beautiful and I can see it all as ugly. I travel to see the land, not the people, and I like the land at night better than the day. I don't want to be a citizen. I just want to live here. Right now I need to go for beauty."

"I'm counting on you," she says again.

"Like ether. Like quicksilver. Like radiation. Like a knife. Like a bullet."

"I mean it."

"I can be sterling. I can drink a six-pack. I can eat gunsmoke and shit cherry bombs."

"We could have officially ended up lovers last night," she says.

"No. Nothing of the kind. When I take you, baby, it will be suddenly, massively and decisively."

"You American boy, you," she says, working her toes into his back.

"I am an American boy," he says.

She sits on his back and gets her knees up, her feet on the floor. She gets her elbows on her knees and her hands over her breasts. She lifts and he rolls over. He looks down and sees the patch of white cotton between her legs, resting on him, perched there like that.

"Redfield," she says. "I have to ask you something. Aside from the obvious, you know, us being related, is there something wrong? I mean, you never even get a little hard."

"I haven't," he says. "Not for a while. Not since the accident."

"Oh," she says, and they stare at each other until finally she shrugs, gives off a tight smile and raises her eyebrows.

"Let's try and eat something," he whispers. "Food, I mean."

They get up and go to the kitchen. Redfield tells Juliet to sit down and he will get food and drink. She watches him walk the floor, watches the muscles slide under his skin.

He stops and points to his knees. He says, Listen, and begins to walk again. His knees sound like crunched up aluminum foil.

"It sounds like it should hurt. Your hurts are starting to piss me off."

He's at the sink gobbling a handful of pills, painkillers.

"My knees used to blow up," he says, "and they'd have to tape them off. No big deal."

She gets in a chair and folds her arms. She's coming to a decision as to whether she wants him around. The pain he carries compounds her own. She shakes her head at how foolish her thoughts can be. She needs him to be here, to stop the echo, to fill the house with his creaking, his groans, his constant jabber. She feels so helpless, so hopeless.

He's speaking again, into the cupboards.

". . . My idea of the perfect life is to go to the grocery once a week and buy stuff for a really great meal, maybe fajitas or pesto or tacos or pizza or hamburgers or trout or steak or lasagna. So I cook it up for her and feed her and after a really long time, I eat her alive. She screams with pleasure and tells me to keep on eating, to eat her up, to eat her alive. Tonight I will make for you Salsa Juliet."

Tonight, she wonders. When is tonight? What is to-

night? He's like a child. Everything in the past was yesterday. Everything in the future is tomorrow. When there is
no time, there is a prolonging of guilt, of scarlet shame,
scarlet like chilies drying in the sun. She patches words
into her head. She strings them in a rosary, a squash
blossom rosary. Again, she feels the wings in her stomach. Her mind goes searching for her child. What have I
gone and done? How can I ever make it better?

". . . I want a place to rest. I want a home of my own.
I'm a hard-luck kind of guy. I feel like life is something
else, some other thing that's out there. Something I don't
have and it's stalking me, turned on me like a bad dog.
One time I am pounding down the New York State
T-way and a sheet of plywood blows off a truck way up
in front of me and it comes wafting back through the air,
slicing, diving, floating. It covered both lanes in its flight
and I couldn't avoid it. So I just sucked it up and kept on
going. When it got to me, a corner of it nicked my finger.
Four foot by eight foot and a corner of it gets my little
finger. I'd ducked down my chin on the tank. It was
going to hit me. I sure as hell didn't want to be decapi-
tated. So it hit my little finger and peeled it straight back.
I am dangerous to myself because I have this condition
where I don't feel pain in any little way."

Redfield takes up a handful of cilantro and keeps it to
his face. He breathes its scent, smiling. He knows she
wants to get inside him a little bit. She wants to settle
him, wants to use his past to connect him to her, connect
him to himself. His mind flees, arcing off the surface of
his brain, sending sparks wherever it touches down.

There is so much he doesn't want to remember. He knows she's had a really big time in life and she's coming off it. It's like there's been a death in the family of herself. He wants her to tell him what it is, but he can't shut up long enough for her to do it.

"I was carrying this pistol before because I was going to make the run through New Jersey and I'd read in the paper where these guys were rear-ending out-of-state cars late at night and then when the people pulled over they were being robbed. I thought, Them sons a bitches aren't going to get me. You see, I'd have that pistol on my lap and when they came up to the car I'd roll down the window, hear what they had to say, then shoot them right through the door."

She hears herself. "How can you even imagine doing that?"

"I know what you mean. You could go a little deaf if you did it too often—and those car doors, they ain't cheap. Besides, I was on the bike."

Her breath shortens. She wants to tell him to stop for a while. She wants to fold up, to curl away like burning paper.

"So I pulled into the Vince Lombardi Service Area to get some gas," he says, "and there was this guy there who just took his time. He ignored me at first, walked slow, looked at me like I was nothing. I tried to be nice. I said, Hello and how are you, but he kept looking at me like I was shit, boring shit that didn't even matter to him, and I wanted to kill him."

"God, Ray, you did kill somebody back East."

"No. No. But I felt like it. I still feel like it's something I want to do. I get this rage that just washes over me. So I go into the coffee shop and there's Vince looking up at me with that shit-eating grin on his face, that space between his teeth. He's looking up at me from an ashtray and I look some more and everything is ashtrays. There's the other world out there. We do not know what it is. We cannot break through. Everything we say, everything we do. Did you know that four fifths of taste is smell?"

"Jesus, Redfield. You're a perfect example of how a little education is a bad thing."

"I took a whole semester. Intro to Soc., Intro to Psych., Intro Hist., Intro Eng. and Intro Philosophy. Intro to my dick. I learned *all* the words. I learned what they mean. I learned the cutting issues of the day. I learned what *postmodern* and *deconstruction* mean."

"What's it mean?"

"I can't tell you. I'm sworn to secrecy."

"A lot of words are just made up."

"A lot of made-up words. I want to know the words for real things. Stilson wrench, spandrel, whorled milkweed, malachite, Malawi, nikubori, dreidel."

"They're just names for things."

"Look at these damn names we're stuck with."

"I like my name."

"Yeah, that's because you didn't have some asshole gym teacher in the seventh grade make fun of it."

"It could be worse. You could be a boy named Sue."

"Right, sue me."

He's striding the tiles, flexing and sweating. His eyes go black and she can tell there are surges in his body.

"Why do you want to be like this," she says.

"I don't know what I want to be. I only know what I don't want to be."

"What don't you want to be?"

"I don't want to be weak or reasonable."

Redfield tells her to wait where she is and lumbers off down the hall. When he comes back he has a shiny black half helmet still wrapped in plastic.

"For you," he says. "I bought it for you in case you wanted to travel a little."

"No," she says. "I can't go. I can't ever leave here."

"Like never?"

She pulls her knees to her chest and wraps her arms around them. Her face says never, says that's a horrifying thought.

He reads her, sees the thought of leaving here is a knife inside her.

"Fuck it, then," he says, winging the helmet across the kitchen, knocking out the toaster oven, sending it all to smash on the floor.

8

A man comes by late that night. He was passing through and thought he'd stop in to say hello. He asks if Karen is in. How long has she been gone? Has it been that long? Do you know where she went to? Just disappeared.

Redfield politely turns him away and goes to Juliet.

"The bastards," he says.

"Please don't talk about them that way. Before you came, they were the only company I had. I'd invite them in and we'd have coffee and I'd always have a little something for them to eat, because sometimes they'd be hungry or drunk. They are always related to her or went to college with her or some story."

"That wasn't just a little dangerous, was it?"

"I had a girl's life. Poor self-image, low expectations and little confidence. I yearned for companionship."

"No. Not you. Say it ain't so."

"Besides, I'd always get out something to cut up with the chef's knife. I'd feed them celery and carrots. I'd keep cutting, *chunk, chunk,* until they got around to showing me pictures of their kids. I took that to mean the danger had passed."

"Who do you think this Karen was?"

"One of the guys fessed up. He told me this house used to be run by her. At night men would come and pay her to do the sex thing with one of her girls. The girls would stay for two weeks at a time before moving on to Flagstaff or Amarillo. They were girls who couldn't make it in Vegas anymore. Everything was on the up and up. They went for the older-lady-next-door kind of scene. Then the house got swept up in a savings-and-loan deal and now it's kind of in limbo.

"We are sorry about earlier, aren't we—about the toaster oven?"

"Yes we are," Redfield says.

★

The next night another man comes by. Redfield isn't there to get the door. He left early in the morning. He said, To see a man south of Clovis named Rip. He went to see about a job. Juliet didn't want him to leave but didn't say anything. She didn't ask him to stay or take her with him. Now she's climbing the walls. He should've been back long ago. She's afraid he'll never come back.

She knows this man. It's Rick. He's brought her a box of raspberry tea. Rick is married to Lorelai and they're the new parents of her baby. She found them in the classifieds: *Loving, childless couple long to provide white newborn with lifetime commitment of endless love, security and educational opportunities. Tennis courts, pool and fireplace. Legal and medical expenses paid. Call Rick and Lorelai. Call collect.*

They were just up from a classified for the romance hotline: *Romance is back in your area. Don't just dream. Successful since 1972. Three dollars for the first minute.*

So she flew to Albuquerque and Rick put her up in this house his company was holding. She spent time with Lorelai. They went to childbirth classes together. Lorelai was her coach and felt just as pregnant as Juliet.

Afterward, they weren't so loving. She rested for a few days. A counselor told her about postpartum perplexity syndrome, said words like *schizo-affective, atypical psychotic reaction, reactive psychosis* and made her write them down. Take notes like in school. Spoke to her as if she were a pet or dumb in a pleasant way. Told her Rick and Lorelai had adoption insurance. Told her not to have any funny ideas. Smiling. Then Rick took her to the airport. He put her on an airplane, but something was wrong with one of the engines, so they taxied off the runway and back to the terminal. They said they'd bring up another plane and all the passengers would be transferred in time. Either that or they could have a ticket to anywhere, anytime. Transferred in time, she thought, and decided to take the ticket to anywhere, anytime and caught a taxi back to the house. She told them she wanted to stay a little longer, and Lorelai said it would be okay.

"We have to talk," Rick says.

She's been expecting this. She's been here almost a month, since she gave birth. Her pelvis begins to ache. She hasn't used her heating pad since Redfield arrived. Where has he gone? Why isn't he here?

"Come sit down," she says, the words escaping with her breath.

They sit in the living room. The last time Rick wanted to talk, he told her Lorelai was experiencing insomnia. She was emotionally labile and experiencing auditory hallucinations. He asked if he could put his head in her lap. She said, I don't think so.

She offers him something to drink, maybe some food, but he declines.

"Juliet," he begins. "We have to talk about your plans."

"Please," she says. "Do we have to? I am very sad at this moment. I understand everything, I really do. I just need a little bit of time. Please don't worry about me. I'm waiting for a friend to come back."

She can see the look on his face. He misunderstood her last sentence. He's college-educated, his mind prone to metaphor. He must think she's crazy. She shakes her head. She didn't want to be so honest with him about herself. She feels again the loss that lived with her before Redfield filled the house with his talk.

"It's my emotions," she says. "They're all fucked up right now. I don't know up from down, over from under. You want the truth?"

She waits for him to show he wants the truth, and then she speaks. Her words are steady and gain conviction.

"I try to pretend none of this ever happened. I numb myself to everything in my life. I'm afraid to make decisions."

That is truth, she thinks. Those are the words she's been looking for.

Rick clasps his hands. He looks at the floor and then into space. She can see he's rearranging sentences in his head, choosing his words wisely.

"Juliet," he says slowly, calmly, almost a whisper. "Juliet, no matter how bad a stress situation seems, you can rephrase it to find something positive about the experience and get through the stress of the moment. It's a way of finding good in any situation of life."

She can feel the room slipping out from under her. Inside she feels like iron, like she could kill this man with her bare hands. She thinks the sinking feeling she's having must be the room itself. It can't be me. She eyes him and takes a breath.

"Okay," she says. "Here goes. A man I loved intensely fucked me over so bad, I sold my baby to you and now

I feel like the stupid whore of the universe. I have, as they say, transgressed."

"You're depressed."

"Fuck you too."

"You have to rephrase this. We're talking about your self-esteem. Self-esteem is the feel-good about yourself that comes from healthy self-love. Feeling good about yourself is the foundation of all loving relationships. You cannot accept love without feeling worthy of being loved."

"What does that mean?" she asks, starting to cry. "What does that mean?"

"I came to tell you that we've sold this house."

She nods her head. The iron she once felt goes cold and brittle inside her. He's telling her it's time to leave, time to go away.

"Look, Juliet. This isn't easy for us, either. We're having a lot of adjustments to cope with."

"How long do I have?"

"No rush," he says. "Three or four weeks, and no matter what, I want you to know that Lorelai and I will always love you for the gift you've given us."

Rick gets up. He shakes his right leg to straighten the crease in his trousers, bends the other knee. He walks to the door, and Juliet follows. He reaches out to take her hand, but she looks away.

He sighs and tells her, "Oh, one more thing. Lorelai thinks her milk will come in. It's remarkable. She thought you'd be happy to know."

Juliet closes the door and sits in the dark waiting for

Redfield. She's come to realize something horrible, but her mind won't deliver up the words for it and so she's saved from knowing what it is. It's just a feeling she has that burns, a feeling that cuts away inside her.

She thinks, I will forever be a woman who has company.

★

Redfield sits out on the patio, his boots square on a flagstone he's just replaced. He's waiting for the man to leave. In the light of the night he can see to the east Sandia Crest, a hump of mountain that has its own weather, seems so close to touch. It was the home of Sandia man, maybe the earliest American, twenty-five thousand years ago. He chose a deep hole high in the wall of Los Huertas Canyon on the northeast slope. He came hunting wolves and saber-toothed cats, left behind flaked stone.

He's tired, his mind 'bout conked out, but all senses on full speed. He's just back from a land where the wind comes of its own accord, a land of dirt roads and rusty cattle guards, taut strands of barbed wire, a John Deere dealership, a coffee shop.

It's 600,000 acres New Mexico lost to Texas because a surveyor in 1859 couldn't find the 103rd meridian, so he drew the state line two miles west of where it should've been.

He watches the man with Juliet inside the house, wonders if the man is friend or foe, wonders if they'll touch, wonders if he'll have to drive through the window and kill the man, likes that as a possibility.

Redfield had been to see a man named Rip. He had trouble finding him. He'd gotten the directions from a guy in Memphis named Fast. He wrote them on the back of a ten-dollar bill and couldn't find it. It isn't smart to go looking for people like Rip.

But Redfield remembered enough to get him down miles of dusty road until a double-wide in the middle of nothing hove into view.

The air smelled like cat piss on gardenias. Rip had been told Redfield might come by. He put down his scattergun and walked out into the sun. He smiled and waved. Redfield waved back, taking note of the dynamite Rip wore strapped to his waist. Rip was a cook. He made pure Texas grit and now it sits under the stone, under his boots.

Every night the lightning has come, some in jags of light reflected under a hood of clouds, others just lightning. The mountain makes the weather here, lightning, wind, thunder, sun, the blue sky.

She sees him and comes out to where he is.

"You missed our company."

"I saw him. It's why I didn't come in."

"Did you have a nice time?"

"I'm leaving tomorrow."

"You can't," she says, fighting not to plead.

"What do you mean I can't?"

"Where are you going?"

"Out to the state of California. My father took this trip in 1948 and he always talked about it like it was a big part of his life. I'm going to stop along the way where he stopped and then stay awhile and then work my way back home, I guess. That is, if I don't get famous."

Juliet catches herself fretting. She's twining her fingers and plucking at her hair. Stop it, she thinks. Stop it.

She says, "Our lives are not this bad, are they? I mean there's been a lot of years. When you look at it this way, it gets stacked up. We shouldn't get the wrong idea about our lives. We only hurt ourselves as if it could save us."

"Do you mind if I ask just what the hell you're doing out here?"

"I came out here to be a sky artist. To be a sky artist, you must study the anatomy of clouds. Cardinals are sacred out here."

She looks to the space between them, wondering whose words those were. Who said them? Did she just say them?

"I have to go and I have to stay," she says.

He goes to her and gets his hands on her shoulders. He thinks to shake her, but he doesn't. He squeezes until he sees the lift of pain in her eyes.

"Juliet. I may be fucked up, but I'm not real stupid. Tell me the truth. I thought you came out here to study jewelry making. Put some rock salt in a test tube, cork it and call it a crystal. Sell it in Connecticut. What's the story? You dump that loser back East for this loser out West?"

He feels her go weak in his hands. He knows she'll fall if he doesn't hold her.

"I want to go for a walk," she whispers.

They go out the gate and disappear into the bosque. They cross the acequias, irrigation ditches leaking water onto the fields of vegetables, millet, sorghum, alfalfa, landscape trees, ornamentals.

They stand on the banks of the river, their heels in sand, and watch a faraway storm. Further down are jetty jacks, channel steel cabled together in tripods, designed to catch logs and save homes when the river sprawls its banks. Now they're obsolete, but without the floods the cottonwoods will die, no trauma to scar open their seeds.

There is no sound before them. The river is flat and smooth, making its sweep south. The silence of the river and the mountain seems to outweigh them, levitate them.

"The lightning is like flashbulbs. It's like a war," Juliet says. "That cloud looks like a mushroom cloud."

"Yeah, mushroom cloud, electricity, flashbulb, war. Why can't it just be lightning?"

"I need to bring art into my life."

"Art? I knew a guy named Art."

"The ditches we crossed. They're haunted by a witch named Yolanda Dora. She's the ditch witch. She snatches children and they disappear."

"Really?"

"Yes. Children get lost in the bosque and when they can't be found, people say it was Yolanda Dora."

"What does she look like?"

"She looks like the kind of person who'd snatch children. Redfield, the truth is I came out here because I was pregnant. I gave my baby away and that's just what I've gone and done."

"Is that who was here tonight?"

"Yes."

Redfield can feel his body making adjustments to keep him on his feet, huge stones shifting inside him, hydraulics, steady and incremental movement.

"This has been the best year and worst year of my life, a time for fuck-ups. How could I do something so wrong? And end up getting money for it?"

"You must have the Midas touch."

"Not funny, Ray."

"Sorry."

He lets his hands cup her shoulders and pulls her to his chest. She comes into him, her body rigid.

"The bastards," he says.

"Please don't talk about them like that. They're the parents of my child."

She lets go in his arms and her knees knock into his legs and now he's holding her up.

"They videotaped the birth," she says. She pauses, caught up in thought. Her mind sweeping through details. She repeats herself and then she begins to cry.

"If I come, will you try to be good? Stay out of trouble?"

"Yes."

"Then take me," she tells him. "Take me with you?"

He doesn't answer her.

"If you ever leave me again, I'll kill myself."

He knows he will. Knew he would before she even asked.

"We can only take a few things with us, so choose wisely."

"Of course. I have a history of that."

★

They left late at noon the next day.

Juliet rode behind him gripping handfuls of his leather jacket. She didn't know what she was looking for, didn't even know to look. When she had the baby, the final contraction clenched off her past and then the moment they let her hold it, a new history began to write itself, but it was short.

To the south was the blackness of bad weather, miles away, the monsoons.

CHAPTER

He might've stopped here, Redfield thinks. Might've stopped to take a leak. He was dashing west for the first time like I am. I'm a little older, carry a little more with me, but in reenacting his life, I am acting my own.

Juliet holds on to him, blithe and carefree. She thinks she will come to own this feeling. She'll be a fey creature with a young lover who'll fear for her. Yes, that's what she'll do. She'll leave open this wound forever, like a soldier carries his combat, like a cancer patient carries remission.

Coming out of Thoreau they see how the storm has

wheeled north and now is in front of them. They ride into its maw, praying they won't get wet. They don't know there are tornado warnings, but the knowing wouldn't have stopped them. Redfield has a place he wants to get to and Juliet has a place she wants away from for now and that's what drives them.

Rainbows come and go, double ones, a triple one, rainbows striped across black clouds. Then the raindrops come like bullets.

They pull under a bridge and climb the concrete bank to wait it out. Already, life on the road has a way of giving to them.

"Why didn't you tell me the truth?" Redfield says, as if it's still something to talk about.

Juliet looks down into the highway. Me and the big rigs, she thinks. My life amongst the big rigs. She turns to him and speaks slowly, her word sharpening across her teeth.

"Oh great. You fucker. When was I going to? How was I going to? You've been prattling away for days. Chain-talking like you're crazy. You can be like the rest of them if you want. I tell you something and you wonder why I didn't tell you before. Is my sin truth-telling or timing?"

"Well, good. Now that's an answer."

Redfield stands and bangs his head on a steel beam. He turns to it and stares as if wondering who put it there. He stomps his feet, makes muscles in his arms and shakes his head at her. Then with long strides he goes down the embankment and takes a water bottle from his pack. She can see him gobbling pills. He struts along the shoulder, staying inside the dry.

"I'm sorry," she yells down to him. "I'm sorry."

"When you lose your cherry, you learn to lose," he yells back, neither of them knowing what he meant.

He keeps pacing until the rain stops, then he straddles the bike. She comes down the embankment and slides in behind him.

"Let's be gone," he yells, and they are.

They ride through the Zuñi Mountains over new dry road, but their rain luck runs out in Gallup, so they pull into the El Rancho for the night. The rooms are named after actors and actresses. They get the Lucille Ball room. The placemats in the restaurant recount the movies shot there. In 1948 it was *Streets of Laredo,* with William Holden and William Bendix. Redfield remembers his father singing the song to himself. However fine a thread to that past, he holds to it, tenderly, so as to keep it from breaking. He wants to tell Juliet, but since the bridge they haven't been talking.

Juliet sits across from him, her head nodding as she falls into sleep. She thinks she's falling and sits up abruptly, knocking over her water glass.

She doesn't remember how she got in bed, she only remembers waking up and, chilled by the air conditioner, reaching for a blanket.

Redfield isn't in the room. She looks at the clock. It's past midnight. She pulls the covers over her nose. She remembers the church people telling her, Take the God out of good and you're left with zero. They are words she can't shake. She thinks about her airline ticket. She can go anywhere anytime she wants. By the phone there's a postcard of the desert. On the back it says, *It is so beautiful out here. I am so sorry for what I have done. Leaving you the way I did. I will never be able to make it up to you.*

She studies the handwriting. She thinks it to be her own, but she isn't sure. What if it isn't hers?

She gets so alone she starts to cry. Oh God, where is Redfield?

When he comes back he smells of liquor and smoke. He tells her he had to get some gas, tells her he met up with the drunks of Gallup.

"Tomorrow will be a long ride," he says. "You better get some sleep."

"I don't know if I can keep going. Every day I think it will get better, but every day the feeling of emptiness is new and full. When I was pregnant, I wondered what it'd feel like when someone'd put my baby in my arms and say, Congratulations, you're a mother."

Redfield waits a long time before saying anything, decides he doesn't know what to say, doesn't even know if he's supposed to say anything.

"Your boyfriend?"

"We were going to get married and at the last minute he backed out."

Redfield gets off his bed and goes to her. He lies down next to her. She feels his weight trapping her under the blanket and begins to struggle. He pulls her free and takes her to his chest. She can feel herself sinking into him, a freefall she doesn't want to stop. Finally, she settles and sighs. Redfield strokes her cheek, strokes her into restless sleep, sleep more fitful, more haunted, more labored than the sleep of detox. He holds her while she makes him black and blue. He realizes that no matter what, he can never come to know what she knows.

In the morning they try again, bound for the Grand Canyon, Juliet determined to let the wind and sun do to her what it does to bone. They take I-40 out of Gallup, running the bed of 66, the mother road, riding at 80 mph over the dry washes, the scrabbled land that couldn't hold water even if it had some.

Great sweeps of reservations to the north and south: Navajo, Zuni and Hopi. Baskets, rugs, kachinas, turquoise, pottery, silver, pawn. Petrified Forest National Park. There are so many of these. They deserve their own national park. Petrified trees, petrified animals, petrified people. *This* broken and crumbling by the forces of erosion was a tree 160 million years ago. The Painted Desert, gone red from oxides of iron. The sloping pediments and alluvial fans scored with shallow dry braided stream washes. Logs of agate and jasper.

Redfield spent last night with the drunks of Gallup, Navajos and Hopis and old-timers, prospectors, speculators, mechanics, teachers and missionaries. People who drink. A one-armed Navajo doing pushups for beer, doing pushups with a woman on his back for hard liquor. Inlay channelwork traded in to keep a bar tab alive. There are those who only watch, who think life is a scenic turnout.

When he got back to the Rancho Motel, Juliet was petrified. She'd gone numb with some horror and it wasn't too hard to figure out what, even for a dumb boy like him.

Redfield sighs and even in the wind at 80 mph she can feel him. She squeezes to let him know she's all right, for now.

Holbrook, then Winslow, where they stop for gas and coffee. They sit on on the curb under the west wall of a building where it's a precious few degrees cooler. They hold hands. They don't talk. Redfield thinks about being mature and Juliet thinks about not thinking.

"Look," Redfield says, jumping up. " 'Standing on a corner in Winslow, Arizona.' "

"Yes," she says, brightening. "The song. This is the place. Oh, Redfield, this is the place."

Redfield takes out a stack of two-by-three black-and-whites. They say: *February 12, 1948 picture of the San Francisco Peaks near Flagstaff, Arizona*; *February 12, 1948 San Francisco Peaks near Flagstaff* and *Flagstaff, Arizona*. The pictures are of mountains and trees, the land white with snow. One he doesn't show. He only laughs.

"We have to find these places," he says, tucking away the black-and-whites.

"Redfield, they could be anywhere."

"It tells where they are."

"Yes I know, but . . ."

"Don't you know how important it is to find them?"

"We'll find them."

They head for Flagstaff, leaving behind the piñon and juniper, the creosote bush and smoke tree. Then north through the Kaibab National Forest to Yavapai Point on the South Rim. The run to the Canyon is a climb, but the road is clean and clear, with wide shoulders, plenty of time and tar to take six or eight cars, a parade of campers and buses, time to cut a profile at the crank of a wrist, riding a wave of roadway between rolling expanses, the squared forests of yellow pine and Douglas fir, *the land of many uses.* Ascending the Mogollon Plateau.

Redfield settles in behind a Harley from Indiana pulling a homemade trailer. There's a man and a woman in the saddle, dressed in black leather. He thinks about naming his bike. He remembers his father has a knee that gives out. He wants to make it all better for Juliet because she's his cousin and he loves her. He reaches down to feel her leg, to make sure she's there. These are the thoughts you have on a bike. These are the things you do.

★

On the South Rim there are many who have come to see the Grand Canyon, to see two million years of geologic time. There are families and couples and honeymooners. There are kids and busloads of people. There are bikers flying a Swedish flag and bikers with no flags. There are boys from Japan riding crotch rockets and Danes on Sportsters. They flew into Denver, bought their bikes and are touring America by land. Some are friendly. Some aren't.

Redfield shuts down the motor and they stretch. They feel the resting heat. Redfield looks for the biker he followed in but can't find him. He asks Juliet if she sees them, but she only shakes her head.

Redfield takes out his father's photographs. They say: *You can see where this one was taken. That's ice on the road by the way, Deer at G.C., That's me in car.; February 12, 1948 This is one with a deer at Grand Canyon. He didn't stay long because I didn't have anything to give him. They had about five there all of them were friendly as hell—cute too.; Feb. 12, 1948 Part of Grand Canyon. That is the Colorado river taken through the telescope you see me looking thru. It's about 4 or 5 miles down from where we were.; Feb. 12, 1948 Standing on the edge of G.C. That's about a mile drop six inches in back of me.*

His father is in the Nash; he's on the rim; he holds his hand out to a deer; he stands under a sign. His eye is behind the rest. His hand has been on the back of each for more than forty years.

They walk the rim until they find the spot where they think Redfield's father stood. It's the best spot. He wants Juliet to take his picture.

People crowd the rail with cameras and camcorders. This sets Redfield off on a talking jag.

"Video cameras," he says. "Video cameras. I don't get it. Videotaping the Grand Canyon. It isn't moving. It isn't going anywhere. It's still, isn't it? Like death. Still like death."

He yells, throwing his arms in the air, whipping his hands. Juliet grabs his belt and tells him it's no big deal, they only want to get the whole Canyon.

"The whole Canyon? The whole Canyon. How the hell can you get the whole Canyon? The Canyon isn't a hole. It's a canyon. These people are robbing little pieces of its time. That's what they're doing. It's theft. They are fools. Hey," he yells. "You are all fools. Why don't you all go home and spray-paint lawn furniture."

People stare at him and some walk the other way. Juliet endures. She stops listening. She freezes a smile on her face and lets him keep going.

He jumps to the top rail and stands on the black steel inch-and-a-half pipe, balancing between a three-foot drop and a five-thousand-foot drop, but one with many rocks to break the fall. Juliet starts snapping pictures.

"Okay," Redfield yells. "Give me your attention." He whistles. *"We're going to fill this in.* I want you all to get in a line and start passing rocks up to me. We're going to fill in this hole."

People gasp and point and then turn away. The video cameras turn on him. Down the rail they lean over to get new angles.

"Juliet," he yells. "Get the women together and make some bologna sandwiches. This could take a while. We might get hungry. Some water jugs, too. We'll need water in this heat to keep up a good steady pace."

Redfield looks behind him, looks down the five thousand feet, feels it singing giddy into his head, the vertigo waltz. The young stream Colorado River runs a thread of silver filament through his brain. He looks back to Juliet. He's yelling. He's walking the rail. Juliet thinks of her baby, doesn't know why at such a moment.

"We shouldn't be here," she whispers.

"Maybe they do this with mirrors," he yells. "Maybe this isn't such a big deal after all. God did this, so what's the big deal? God can do anything he damn well pleases because he's God and God is big."

He looks down again, then across the Canyon through the thick hot updrafts to the North Rim. The earth that is the Canyon undulates in the heat. Bands of purple, mauve, salmon and gray bask in the sun, go black in the cloud shadows. Down there the feel, the sound, of dull thundering impacts as huge boulders roll over and over on the channel bottom in the swift rapids of the river's hydraulic action. America cracked open and he's on the hull. He's yelling.

"Hey, everybody, I got a better idea. Let's go down there and kick some ass. We'll board a raft and steal their women. Those damn rafters really piss me off. You always see them on TV having so much fun. Well, they can kiss my ass."

He stops talking and looks down again. Cameras are snapping along the rail. People are having dreams of the future: *If only he'd fall. Videotape at 11:00. Not for young viewers. Move over, Rodney King. America has a new star, America's Frightening Home Videos.*

Winks and whispers . . . and now here's the tape of the

vacation me and Herby took to the Grand Canyon . . . pan, focus, closeup, man in leather jacket on rail, man leaping from rail, man airborne. Go back, Herby. Rewind. There. Pause. See that. See his right hand. See him giving my Herby the finger? The nerve of some people.

"Come along now," Juliet says, going up to him and taking his hand as if it were glass. "Come down from there. We have enough pictures."

Her mind cants back and forth to thoughts of him coming down and thoughts of him falling. There are flashes of pain and flashes of amazement. There is sadness and objective sadness. There is oblique love, felt love, obscured love.

"Come down," she says, tossing her head and stamping her foot.

Redfield looks at her, the tears coming to his eyes in the place where his father stood.

"Fucking awesome," he whispers. "The G.C. is fucking awesome."

★

Later, the sun refusing to be caught, they pick up real Route 66 out of Seligman, Arizona. The light sparks off the land while at other moments it lays down sheets of gold and fingers of darkness.

They pass through Yampai and Peach Springs, an abandoned Mobil station with its red Pegasus poised for altitude. Down through the Truxton Wash and the Hualapai Reservation and that's where they see the first people, mothers and children walking alongside the road. They wave and Redfield and Juliet wave back. She makes it up in her head they know who she is. I want to stay here, she thinks. I want to stay with these people.

They pull over and Redfield takes out one of the Arizona photographs.

" 'February 12,' " he reads. " 'Me in cactus country. Arizona.' "

The other one, the one he held back before, he looks at but doesn't read. Instead, he says, "So true, so blue."

He gets off the bike and runs off into the desert until he comes to a fence. He props his elbow on the steel post and yells, "Take my picture, take my picture."

There are vultures in the sky, a column of twenty or thirty. They gyre in the air they find. She takes their picture, too.

They ride on. West and west and west.

Juliet is exhausted and luxuriates in her body's dull aches. She's hot and cool. Her hands and arms and neck and face prickle with sunburn. For these miles there is no old bad past that can catch up with her. There is no thinking about the giving up or the leaving behind. If at this very moving place the bike reared up and heeled around, she would not have been surprised. The very moving place is where she wants to be no matter what.

The earth is now black and gold. Shadows cut swaths across the land and make you think it's cool under their dark blanket. You can duck your head into darkness or stick out your hand and bathe it in light. It's like being on a horse. Your sense of worth is deceived.

And for Redfield, in forty years he will be older than

his father ever will, but for a time they are out there together, miles from anywhere. And he feels he's closing in on his life, closing in on his own.

While they ride, Juliet fishes the photographs out of his pocket. She cups them in her right hand and reads through to the one he laughed at. It says: *February 12 Arizona same spot only I'm halfway down.*

Halfway down, she thinks. Isn't that the all-time truth.

★

By the time they get to Kingman it's dark. Their faces are burned and the backs of their hands are tracing white with blisters.

She wakes to light, feels the opening inside her. Mornings are always the worst. No, mornings and nights. No, mornings, days and nights, those are times when its the worst. She wonders why else do they call it morning and the wings come awake, begin to flutter.

Redfield is sitting in front of the window with headphones on, the curtains open. People are walking by. He's watching them load their cars with luggage and coolers of ice. He's drumming his thighs with his thumbs. He's tapping his feet and rocking his heels. He's humming. She sees the headphones aren't jacked in. She goes back to sleep.

When she wakes again, he's sitting on the edge of her bed watching *Mr. Wizard*.

Again in a motel, she thinks. The same one. She remembers waking but can't remember having slept. She can only remember the sounds of keys scraping in locks, small avalanches of ice, voices, the throb of air-conditioning like small jet engines.

"You're up," he says. "Mr. Wizard says if you're lost in the woods, put your eye on something distant and walk to it. He's doing a thing right now with a stool and a fan. He gets the fan going fast enough, it looks like it's stopped."

Juliet sits up and stares at the television. She tries to calculate how far she is from Albuquerque. Mr. Wizard has a magnet and iron filings. He's showing lines of force. Then he gets electricity out of a can of sauerkraut. You need two dissimilar metals and an active chemical.

When *Mr. Wizard* is over, Redfield finds the Weather Channel. They're in the hottest spot in America, maybe the world, Kingman, Arizona. He's overjoyed. He wants every day to be marked. He wants the weather to be complicitous as in all good stories.

He takes out black-and-whites of Hoover Dam. The backs say: *Boulder Dam top 726 ft. down*; *Boulder Dam look up*; *Boulder Dam Bottom*; *Mead Lake Looking out from Dam*. He always thought there was such a place as Boulder Dam, but Congress changed the name to Hoover Dam in 1947. His father should have known that.

Juliet watches him shuffle through his black-and-whites. She has pictures, too. She has a giant cactus and a rattlesnake, the Canyon and poppies and another one of the Canyon. The ink on the backs has gone to clouds; the words have bled from one to another. But she knows what they say—*I'm sorry and I'm sorry.*

"When I was a kid," he says, "I tried to find it on the map. According to the picture, it was a big-assed dam, but I couldn't locate it anywhere. This naming is tricky business. If I have learned one thing, it's you have to watch the bastards every step of the way. Trust there is no history and that's a start."

"Didn't your father explain it?"

"He thought it was Boulder Dam, too."

"Redfield, where are we, anyways?"

"In a motel in Kingman, Arizona. The hottest spot in the whole damn universe. It's time to go. Will you wrap me up?"

*

They pick up Route 93 and head north. Road signs are riddled with bullet holes. Cars are overheating and blowing geysers of steam. The red desert soil turns to gray sand and the light comes like a plate across your nose. There's dusty piñon and juniper, beautiful cactus, scorpions and sidewinders, cholla and prickly pear, ocotillo and creosote bush, rare and distant fulgurites, sand struck to silica glass cylinders shaped like tree roots, petrified lightning-melted sand.

Up through Householder Pass even the cactus can't

live. The land goes to moonscape, giant craters and cracked mountains so close you can touch them. But it's good road, built on the earth's bedrock. It's slow road and he's a little bit afraid because around each turn there's a roadside crater been excavated or maybe the fat white ass of an overheated camper. They're headed for the corner of Arizona a bit east of where Nevada's shank knifes south.

They make a bend and settle in behind the bikers from Indiana. They're headed for the Dam, too.

The Dam.

It is some wonder of the world. There are people who keep count of such things.

If you want to have one for yourself, you'll need 4,400,000 cubic yards of concrete, 45,000,000 lbs. of rebar, 21,670,000 lbs. of gates and valves, 88,000,000 lbs. of plate steel, 840 miles of pipe and fittings, 18,000,000 lbs. of structural steel and 3,551,000 lbs. of dynamite. For all that you'll receive 3.5 billion kilowatt hours a year, the equivalent of 6 million barrels of oil.

"Son of a bitch," Redfield says. "I really, really want one of these."

"If you're nice, maybe I'll get you one for Christmas."

"Juliet makes a funny."

They stare at the Dam and Lake Mead from the Arizona side. The intake towers stand serenely atop the thirty-foot-diameter steel penstocks. The water is blue come down from the sky. The water is blue come down from Wyoming, Utah, Colorado, New Mexico, Nevada and Arizona. Transmission towers angle off the canyon walls, high-voltage transmission lines to L.A., San Berdoo, Las Vegas, Fort Barstow, Kingman, Needles and Boulder City. The air hums with heat and electricity. You get the feeling that something is going on.

The bikers from Indiana yell to them and wave them over. They have the top to their trailer popped open. Inside there's ice and cold sodas. Without a word the man starts snapping cans and passing out cold drinks. He has a crooked arm.

"Hey, bro, we saw your little act back at the Canyon. Pretty righteous."

They all take long drinks and laugh. Redfield likes the way he talks. Juliet feels the beginning of courage. Meeting people. A new life.

"I'm Asphalt, and this is Ostrich Lady. We're on tour."

Redfield and Juliet introduce themselves, and they shake hands across the open space. Redfield asks about the trailer, and Asphalt begins showing him how he constructed it.

Juliet looks at Ostrich Lady. She can see the head of an Ostrich tattooed to her chest, the long neck rising out of her tank top.

"Ostrich Lady. That's a pretty name," Juliet says.

"I got it up in Sturgis," she says. "I always wanted one. I love the ostrich. It's the largest living bird, like the whale is the largest living mammal."

"It's really pretty."

Ostrich Lady pulls down the neck of her tank top so Juliet can see the rest of her animal. It's blue and gray and covers her left breast, its feet poised above her nipple, ready to run.

"I imagine when I get old, Miss Ostrich will get tall and skinny."

Ostrich Lady laughs at her own joke and then Juliet laughs. She wants Redfield to see the ostrich too, but it isn't her breast to show off.

Redfield, Juliet, Asphalt and Ostrich Lady find the shade of a building, where they sit with their cool drinks.

Asphalt's father, Whitey, built this dam. He and Asphalt's mother, Gert, live outside Boulder City. Asphalt knows everything about this dam. He tells them it can hold 9 trillion gallons of water, enough water to cover the state of Pennsylvania to a depth of one foot.

"It's not a state," Redfield says. "It's a commonwealth."

"What's a commonwealth?"

"Pennsylvania."

"Duh!" Asphalt says, waving his crooked arm, and Ostrich Lady breaks out laughing.

So much laughter, Juliet thinks. Maybe its contagious.

Asphalt sings:

My old man got to build this dam
I got to go to Vietnam
My old man was a hard boiled Cat Skinner
I spend my days smelling paint thinner.

"That's Asphalt's story," Ostrich Lady says. "He's kind of a lot fucked up in the head. He's one of those types who's a fucked-up Vietnam vet, but I love him dearly. This is our fifth or sixth time to the Dam."

"Are you going to take the tour?" Redfield asks. He wants to go down to the power plant. He wants to see what 2 million horsepower looks like.

"Nah. Come to Boulder City with us. We'll get Whitey to come back. He'll give you the real tour, not some polyester strut."

"Asphalt and Whitey love each other," Ostrich Lady says. "It's a wonderful thing to see."

A blue-haired Western woman comes out to meet them. Ostrich Lady gets off the bike and hugs her. The woman isn't very tall. Her head comes to just above Ostrich Lady's breasts.

"Hi, honey," the woman says.

"Hi, Mama Thibeau."

The two women hold each other in the driveway. A man comes around the house, limping along on a cane. He and Asphalt shake hands.

"Mama Thibeau, this is Redfield and Juliet. We met them at the Dam and invited them to bunk for a night. I hope it's okay."

Redfield and Juliet smile and shuffle their feet. Whitey has tearful eyes and keeps dabbing at them with a red bandanna. He's wearing a white sleeveless T-shirt, green work pants and slippers. Fine white hair curls from his arms and chest. Gert has on a tank top, Bermuda shorts and Nikes. She takes Juliet's hand, then hugs her as tightly as Ostrich Lady. Juliet can feel how her breasts aren't real. Whitey calls Redfield son. The smell of burning charcoal winds through the air.

"Mama Thibeau, Asphalt would love a bowl of your ice cream. It's all he's been talking about since we left Indiana. Mother Thibeau makes her own ice cream."

"Ice cream is in the fridge, honey. Whitey, you better put on more chicken. Come along, children, we'll sit out on the patio."

Ostrich Lady and Whitey go inside. Redfield, Juliet and Asphalt follow Gert around back. There's a stone patio under a roof and patio furniture and coolers and a barbecue fashioned from a fifty-gallon drum.

Redfield and Juliet sit quietly, sipping beer. Juliet takes his hand and squeezes to make him squeeze back. At this moment she wants to be folded inside the cool black earth. The miles she can see seem to be slowly wicking her life off through her eyes. Her skin throbs inside her clothes, and where the sun has touched her she feels brittle. Who are these people, she wonders, and why are they so nice? She begins to cry and smiles, amazed at how easily the tears are delivered. Says smoke gets in her eyes.

Whitey brings out more chicken, and Ostrich Lady brings Asphalt a bowl of ice cream.

Ostrich Lady calls for attention and then tells them her famous news. Her daughter Michelle has received a full scholarship to Stanford.

"She's smart's a whip," Asphalt says.

"Oh, honey, that's such good news," Gert says.

"We've known for a while, but we waited so we could see the look on your faces. Shit, I didn't even know where Stanford was."

"That's the greatest," Whitey says, dropping chicken wings onto the grill. "That's a good school."

"Where is she now?" Juliet says.

"Soooo," Ostrich Lady says. "We are on tour of this great land America."

"We are too," Redfield says.

"Where's your daughter now?" Juliet says again, feeling as if she's only a voice.

"Well! That's some news too. My daddy had a 1953 Indian Roadmaster and a 1947 Indian Chief. When he died they became mine. So you know what me and Asphalt did? We took them down to the Antique Motorcycle Auction in Daytona and walked away with over forty thousand dollars in cash money. I said to Asphalt, we are rich, baby doll. We have struck the mother lode."

"How could you sell your father's motorcycles?" Redfield says.

"Because he told me to, darling. I wouldn't have done it if he hadn't told me to. So we are in the pink, so in love. We shut down the shop and are on tour."

"Where is your daughter?"

"With her gramma. We'll meet her in Palo Alto in August."

"She's a whip," Asphalt says. "She has a pornographic memory."

"Photographic!" Ostrich Lady slaps him. "Yours is pornographic."

"Them was beautiful bikes," Whitey says, his upper body wreathed in smoke. "I saw pictures of them."

"The thrill of it all," Asphalt says.

"Oh, honey, your beautiful skin," Ostrich Lady says, going to Juliet. "We're going to have to get you some sunscreen and some aloe gel. I've got aloe lotion, too. It's fifty percent aloe gel and a blend of shea butter, wheat germ and apricot oils . . ."

Ostrich Lady gets up handfuls of Juliet's white hair, strokes her skin with the backs of her fingers.

"It's very soothing, all natural. It'll moisturize your skin. You do have sensitive skin. You should have some leathers. Riding in those clothes will wear you out. The sun will get you. And the wind. Your hair is so white. I'll get my kit."

Ostrich Lady comes back with a nylon sack full of lotions and shampoos. She squeezes moisturizer into her hand and gently rubs it into Juliet's skin, her face, neck, shoulders and arms.

"Medical use of aloe vera dates back thirty-five hundred years. Marco Polo saw the Chinese use it as a medicine and beauty potion. I have extra of everything. You can take some until you get some for yourself. Take this cocoa butter sun lotion. It's really good. It contains cocoa butter, sesame oil, black walnut leaf and aloe vera gel. Use this after your skin gets tanned."

★

More people come to eat chicken. There's Horace and Jane, Tex and Mona, Milt and Jo. They bring potato salads, macaroni salads, baked beans, upside-down cakes and Jell-O molds.

Horace, Tex and Milt worked on the Dam with Whitey from gravel up. Gert was the only woman of the group who'd been there from the start. Milt was a flag-man, Tex a truck driver, Horace a rigger-rodman and Whitey a Cat skinner. From the Dam they left for the service, for big jobs in Michigan, in Quebec, in Colombia, hydro projects, bridges and highways, but it's here where they've come to retire, here where the Dam held them in their orbits, brought them to its home.

Redfield gets them to talk about the Dam while they eat, tells them his father saw the Dam, shows them the pictures.

Milt says: It's big, Boulder Dam or Hoover Dam as they now call it. It employed five thousand men around the clock. Pick-and-shovel work. Laborers made four bucks a day seven days a week and if you didn't want it, there were two hundred boys lined up waiting to take your job.

Horace says: You got two days at Christmas and two days on the Fourth of July.

Redfield says: Those were the days.

So it's like this, Juliet thinks. It goes like this.

Whitey says: They'd hoist me and the Cat with the cableway and set me down onto the shot to muck it off five or six hundred feet up in the air. There was a few times I thought I was going over. I wasn't scared. I had a job and that was that.

Milt says: One day I was flagging and I see a high-scaler fall off the Nevada side. There weren't any trucks coming, so I ran over to help, but he was deader than a mackerel. By that time there were twenty trucks backed up. A hard-boiled super came over and said, What the fuck are you doing? You got twenty trucks backed up.

Jo says: Milt! Watch your mouth.

Milt says: I told him what happened, and he says, Don't worry, he won't hurt nobody.

Tex says: It was better to get hurt in Arizona because the compensation was higher.

Horace says: Yes, but it was better to die in Nevada because if you died in Arizona, the coroner had to come up from Kingman. Took hours.

Whitey brings on another platter of chicken. He carries his cane hooked over his wrist and dabs at his eyes, all the while smiling. He catches Juliet's eye and winks, makes her smile too.

Tex says: I seen one guy break his leg in Nevada and crawl over to Arizona.

Redfield says: My father told me there were men buried in that dam.

Tex says: That's shit! Ninety-six men died on that job and we got every one of them out.

Redfield doesn't listen. He thinks how the Dam was built by men and he likes the thought that some of them are still buried there, because that's what his old man told him.

Tex says: I drove truck. Hard tail. Hard rubber. Hauling earth. It was strictly a high-ball job. Every time I go down there I hold my hand over my heart.

Horace says: We had eight big Manion electric shovels with two yard dippers. Their cables had twenty-three hundred volts running through them. Guys waist-deep in water dragging cables behind those shovels. To this day I can never get over that.

Juliet looks at the women. Jane is staring off into the desert, finger to her cheek. Mona looks at her hands. Jo rubs her forehead, and only Gert seems to be listening, though she's heard it all before. Juliet wonders what it must be like to share your husband with something as big as Hoover Dam. She takes time to appreciate having had that thought. Maybe she will wake from all this. She pinches herself, lets go and watches that patch of skin blossom. Must be this is as awake as it gets. Maybe she should call Albuquerque to see if everything is okay. People are calling each other on the phone all the time.

Asphalt and Ostrich Lady sit off to the side sharing a joint. Ostrich Lady smiles and gives Juliet a wink.

Whitey says: We built factories right on the site. Turned out everything we needed. We had a plate steel fabricating plant. Concrete plant. We'd fire off a ton of dynamite in a single shot. One day alone we drove 256 feet of tunnel. Tunnels so big two freight trains could pass by each other.

Tex says: The ignitions were never shut off. You came on your shift and took your truck on the fly. Big trucks. Tight trucks. Model A Fords used for hauling drill steel.

Horace says: Those high-scalers were up there like monkeys on ropes handling a jackhammer. They'd sit in a little bosun's chair. They knocked a million cubic yards of rock from the canyon walls.

Milt says: We lived in dorms and tent cities. We came from all over the country. We built our own railroad.

Redfield says: The Dam is awesome. It's almost as awesome as the Grand Canyon.

Tex says: God built the Grand Canyon, boy. Men built the fucking Dam.

Mona says: Watch your mouth, Tex.

Jane says: Men are good for just two things, and one of them is building dams.

Gert says: They can clean up, too. I think it's their turn.

★

Nightime in the desert city.

". . . These people live in the desert, in the mountains, at the end roads, past the end of roads. They live under bridges, in parks and alleys, in abandoned cars and schoolbuses. They live alone and behind doors. . . .

Because these people sometimes don't wash, sometimes don't have a home or a job, sometimes are ignorant or psychotic, sometimes break the law, sometimes just want to be left alone, sometimes don't give a shit. Because these people could take something that's yours, say: your money or gold, or a loaf of bread or your VCR, maybe your life, but not likely because they usually kill each other, but this scares you. Mainly, just knowing they're out there scares you. They clutter up the scenery. They sometimes stink and their smell could be in your nose. Hey, I know some of these people and now that I think about it, you should be scared, but not of the children, not yet."

"Asphalt pontificates," Ostrich Lady says.

"You know, man, sometimes I just don't give a shit."

"You are sometimes no day at the beach," Ostrich Lady says.

"Okay. Now, brother Redfield, I'm going to give you an education. You go into California on Route I-15. You go by day and you're okay. You don't wander off that road. You go through Nevada, you keep your ass glued to the mains and you go by day. Utah, too."

"Sure, okay."

"In California you got Fort Irwin, China Lake, Twenty-nine Palms. In Nevada you got Nellis and in Utah you got Wendover. In Arizona you got Yuma and in New Mexico you got White Sands and Fort Bliss. They got these SPEC OPS guys. They're supermen. They ain't on anybody's books except some fuck nut at Langley.

These guys are supermen. They can lift half-tracks. They can run down a car in their bare feet. They do this with pharmaceuticals, little black boxes they implant under the skin. Sometimes these guys go haywire, they go goofongdoo, if you know what I mean. They'll snatch a citizen. Shit, where do you think all these missing children end up? They're being raised to be supermen."

The company has gone home. Gert has gone to bed. Asphalt, Ostrich Lady, Whitey, Juliet and Redfield recline in chaise longues. Warmth now comes from the earth, not the sky. Juliet reaches across to take Redfield's hand. She wants to stick his fingers in her ears. She's way tired, too gone to delight in Asphalt's stories. She rests quietly, feeling her skin from the inside out, feeling how nice the salves of Ostrich Lady. If only, she thinks, if only I can stay this tired the rest of my life.

"So how do you know all this?" Redfield says.

Asphalt looks to Ostrich Lady as if he needs encouragement.

"Go ahead. Tell him," she says, cutting the air with her hand.

"I used to be one. I'm not saying I was like these guys, but I used to be one. Then it was mainly old-fashioned stuff. Pharmacy stuff. Best speed you'll ever see on the streets. They'd place it under your skin in a bolus. You could stay awake all week until finally you'd want to die just for a little rest. Then later there was mind shit. Trying to stimulate brain centers to bring on endorphins and adrenaline. I could see it coming. One day I see a guy pop his fingers through an inch-thick sheet of plywood. Just like that, he walks up to it, smiles and then drives his fingers right through it. Slow like. Like it was butter. So I get real stupid.

"I broke this arm. I did it on purpose. Then I wouldn't let it heal. They'd give me shit for it. Other guy would break stuff. They'd juice 'em up and in three, four days, bones would heal. I'd keep breaking my arm and they couldn't figure it out. I was Mr. Gung ho, but I'd keep dropping further and further back, until they let me drift away. I begged them to let me stay so they wouldn't get wise."

Juliet thinks she wakes, thinks she missed something in Asphalt's story. She rolls her head and squeezes Redfield's hand. Maybe she dozed off. She wants it to happen again.

"I get to be a citizen again. Things went quiet for a long time. I get a little blacktop business going, driveways and small parking lots. I'm wrenching bikes and making runs with the Invaders. I'd hear stories. Then one morning I come downstairs and there's this guy I knew sleeping on my couch. He wouldn't speak. I'd go to work and when I got home he'd be gone, like a ghost, no sign, except for a brand-new hundred-dollar bill sitting on my table. Then this past spring one of them guys is there on the couch and he's a talker. He was over in Saudi. One of them guys who spent weeks at a time riding a dirt bike into Iraq. He'd sleep by day in a hole and ride by night. He tells me he was up too long one night and it started getting light when in front of him, this guy rises up out of the sand. He didn't know who it was, so he veered off and took it up to about fifty to get the hell out of there. This guy starts chasing him on foot. He caught up with him and he's running alongside."

Ostrich Lady interrupts. She tells Juliet that Asphalt went on a drunk and missed the war in the Gulf, so she got him the videotape for Father's Day.

"His communications were out and he needed to get some coordinates into his command. Scud missiles aimed at Israel. Then he disappears into the desert. You read about my friend. When they start letting that stuff out, you know it's because there's a whole lot more to keep secret. They only give out information to get in the way of other information. The friend told me this because he was mad as hell. You see, all this time, he thought he was the baddest motherfucker in the jungle and now he finds he isn't. It was discouraging to him. The next morning he's gone and there's two new hundreds rolled up like joints and they're sticking out of a little mound of sand he dumped on the kitchen table. You hear what I'm telling you?"

"Boy's right," Whitey says. "We had guys in Korea go like whirlwinds. Hand to hand, they'd kill fifteen guys at once. I saw one guy get shot two, three times and it didn't even faze him. Well, time for old Whitey to hit the sack."

The old man gets up and tenderly walks the patio, trying for the blood to perk in his legs. He says goodnight to all, calls Redfield and Asphalt son and kisses the women on the top of their heads.

After Whitey goes to bed, Asphalt gets the blankets Gert left by the sliding door.

They line up the four chaise longues side by side facing east. The women take the middle ones. Asphalt goes inside and comes back with cold chicken, beer and vinegar potato chips. Sounds of eating, sounds of pop-tops snapping in the moonlight.

Redfield feels a great weight descending upon him. In this spot, where his chair sits on the earth, gravity has flared up, gone off the scale. He's thirsty but can barely get the beer to his mouth. He's hungry but the chicken meat is stitched to the bone and he can't separate the two. He's crashing. He doesn't care and he's afraid. His eyes are sensitive to even starlight. He eases his sunglasses off the top of his head and onto his nose. He can hear them eating and drinking, hear it going down, hear digestion.

"Sometimes I think I'm the only woman in America who hasn't been photographed in the nude," Ostrich Lady says. "I want some nude pictures for my history so I can show my grandkids what I used to look like."

"I have a camera," Juliet says, her voice a tease.

"Oh, Asphalt, would you mind if I posed?"

"Walk on, woman."

"Don't be silly," Juliet says. "It's dark."

Redfield mumbles, "There's a lot of women haven't been photographed nude."

But Ostrich Lady is already up and taking off her clothes. Asphalt fires up some smoke and passes it down the line while Ostrich Lady touches herself. She's white in the night, her Ostrich tall and blue.

"I used to be an exotic dancer, didn't I, Asphalt?"

"It's where I met you, baby. You picked me out of the crowd and sat on my lap. Beautiful."

Ostrich Lady dances on the patio. She bumps and grinds. She makes her belly ripple.

Redfield, Juliet and Asphalt frame their fingers in front of their faces. They make clicking sounds and say, One more, one more, now turn around, now the hips, the hands again, hand on your hip . . .

"So beautiful," Juliet says.

★

In the night Juliet wakes up to the sound of Ostrich Lady and Asphalt making love. She looks over and sees Ostrich Lady's rising white back, her hair dropping across her face, a hand on the arm of the chair. She's dancing again.

Juliet lets her knees fall apart. She puts her hand on herself and feels nothing, nothing at all. She tries to remember what it's supposed to feel like, but she can't. She slides her hand up and works her nipple. By the time Ostrich Lady's back arches and stiffens, Juliet's T-shirt is soaked. She crosses her arms and fights her way back into sleep.

Redfield sleeps that night too, the first night in some days. When he wakes it's daylight and Gert is sitting beside him drinking coffee. She tells him that Whitey took the girls into Vegas. Asphalt's in the garage servicing his ride. She pours him a cup of coffee from an urn she has on the table.

"You have been very kind to us," Redfield says.

"Oh, that's all right. It's everybody's sky. Anybody can sleep under it. It's nice having you here. You should see some of the strays those two bring by. Forgive me, but white trash if I do say so myself."

"What did they go into Vegas for?"

"Skin cream, I think."

Redfield clears his throat and sits up in the lounge chair. He rearranges the blanket. He waits for her to notice he wants to get up.

"Oh go ahead and get up," she says. "You haven't got anything that I haven't seen. I'm too old to get up and move just to avoid seeing a naked man."

Redfield likes her. He turns the blanket and sits with his back to her. He finds his jeans on the floor and slips his legs into them, then stands. The bandage he wears around his ribs is loose and dangling, the tension gone out of it. Gert gets up and goes inside. Redfield shuffles to the end of the patio. He gets his fly down and pisses into the cactus. His urine is pink. He shuffles back to the lounge and puts on his socks and boots. The pain is there. He grits his teeth and whimpers. He thinks maybe he should see a doctor, but why bother?

Gert comes out with a wide Ace bandage and a sponge. She calls his name and gestures for him to come to her, to put up his arms. She unwraps the sweaty bandage from his ribs, wrinkling her nose.

"It's getting a little smelly, isn't it?"

"Yes," Redfield whispers, his eyes closed.

She turns on the outside faucet, wets the sponge and bathes his torso. Then she wraps the new bandage around him.

"Thank you," he says.

"I've wrapped up quite a few ribs in my life. If it wasn't those boys down at the Dam working, it was those boys getting hurt while playing. You better go out front, and if you're nice, you can talk my son into changing your oil for you."

Redfield thanks her again and gets his denim shirt on.

"Let me," she says, squaring it on his shoulders and snapping the buttons. "I know you're a good boy. All you boys are."

He turns to walk away and she spanks him on the ass. It's a hard slap, right into his back pocket.

"One to grow on," she says. "You probably need it for something anyways."

Asphalt's in the driveway working on his bike. He has it rolled onto a tarp. Empty oil cans are stacked, draining into each other. Full cans sit beside them. Wrenches and rags are neatly lined up. The smell of oil and coffee fill the dry, hot air. It's going to be another scorcher. It makes your skin fit differently.

"Hey, bro, how can you tell if a woman has brain damage?"

"I don't know," Redfield says.

"I don't either! Get it!"

Asphalt goes into spasms of laughter, tells Redfield he made it up himself.

"You look a little tore up this morning. Look like you got et by a coyote and shit off a cliff, as the saying goes."

"I know. I guess I'm running on empty. Old Tex got a little cranked up last night, didn't he?"

"Par for the course. Par for the course. But I'll tell you, mister, you don't fuck with Whitey. Man's iron, steel and grit. You don't fuck with his kid, either."

"Energy that just ain't there."

"Sometimes you die."

"You wouldn't be holding, would you?"

"I eat it, snort it and smoke, but I don't fire that shit no more. One time I stayed awake for twenty-eight days. It was a good thing, too. I took apart every appliance in the house and then I had to put them all back together again. Everything worked. Slept for five days after that."

"You wouldn't have anything on you?"

Asphalt looks at him and smiles, shaking his head. Then he picks up a screwdriver and pops open his headlight. He takes out a packet, pages of a magazine folded into a small tight square and fastened with a rubber band. He unfolds the paper.

"Are you tough?"

"Tough enough."

He tips the contents, white powder, into Redfield's coffee.

"That oughta be good for a day and a half. It's good stuff. Make you fuck all night."

Redfield slugs down the coffee. What creeps up on him is a kick in the ass that makes him grab for the top of his head. A thunderbolt of sorts from his nose to his toes. Blood slams his heart and sweat leaks from him.

"Oh boy," he says.

★

They're dripping gasoline onto their hands when Whitey pulls in. They've long since finished with the bikes and swept the driveway. They cleaned the garage, too, and painted the long picnic table and creosoted the rail fence. They dug water line for sprinkling the lawn and ordered the pipe. They found a rubber ball and played catch, throwing it over the roof to each other. Redfield is now loving the cool vaporous feel of the gasoline on his skin, the way it makes cuts and nicks blossom red.

Juliet gets out of the car and strikes a pose. She's wearing leather gloves, motorcycle jacket, chaps and a pair of lizard-skin Tony Llamas. All in black.

"Nice," Redfield says. "Very nice."

Ostrich Lady unzips her jacket and pulls it wide. She's wearing a black T-shirt. There's the picture of a woman's backside. She's on her knees, wearing black fishnet stockings with seams up the back. Her dress is flipped over her hips and you can see the soles of her high heels. Beside her the words *Make Friends the Hollywood Way, Fuck 'em*.

The women turn around. Squares have been cut from

their jeans, behind their knees and from the place where leg turns into ass. The bottom third of their back pockets are gone.

"Quite artistic," Asphalt says.

"Whitey got cigars from Nicaragua," Ostrich Lady says. "He's such a rascal. Full of vinegar."

Whitey rolls a fat corona between his lips. He grins like he's high stakes, a roulette maven, and these are his pretty girls.

Redfield can glimpse him in his younger days, jumping down from the big cable-driven Cat and heading home to Gert. She showers him under the hose and after beer, after casserole, after the radio goes silent, they get hot and sweat on each other.

"We went to the Liberace museum," Juliet says. "Chopin's piano was there, and a fifty-pound rhinestone. I don't remember much else that glittered."

Redfield can feel his body hum. He can hear inaudible desert sound, sand shifting, desert bighorn sheep off in the mountains. He can hear freight cars of electricity running through high voltage wires, the water piping under the streets. He can hear the sound of everything shrinking in the heat. The heat is it.

"Well," he says, "time to cut a trail."

"Yes it is," Juliet says, a little sadly. "You all have been so kind."

Ostrich Lady kisses Redfield on the mouth and hugs him. Her mouth close to his ear, she says, "Listen, buster, you take care of that girl. She's been through hell and needs you to be there for her. Now, take care of her or I'll hunt you down."

She kisses him again and smiles, tears in her eyes.

"Listen, bud," Asphalt says. "You avoid Fort Barstow and do not dally in ol' San Berdoo. You hear what I'm telling you?"

Redfield nods his head and shakes hands all around. He turns on the electricity behind his eyes, gives off his most fried look. Then he gets on the Harley and fires it up. Juliet swings in behind him and they putt on down the road.

Ｔhere's a wind that blows up Route 15. It gusts across the dry lakebeds, mesas and wild horse canyons, sculpting them, buffing them, carrying away their infinite particles to another formation, another depression.

Furnace time. They leave Boulder City and descend on L.A. That hot wind is blowing in their direction. It's coming northeast, meeting them every mile. Casinos in the desert like oases, like Taj Mahal, like Angkor Wat, like Thebes, like the Vatican with gas pumps.

A trucker tells them it blows all the time. Like an

exhaust, he says. They take off their helmets at the state line. Juliet gets out her supply of sunblock. North is Death Valley and to the south is the Mojave Desert. Truck brakes chirp and hiss. And here is China Naval Weapons Base, Fort Irwin, Twenty-nine Palms and Fort Edwards, 3 million acres of playground for the well-armed and dangerous. These are the first people to take root here in six hundred years. We don't just forget our pasts, we seal them up, make bombing runs, convert their mass to energy, confuse technology and history, prefer the one and shun the other. Figure what's right for you, then figure out what's right.

Redfield pulls over for gas and liquids. Juliet stays with the bike, says she wants to be alone a little bit, says, Bring me back something. Inside there's a woman he looks at for too long. He makes eye contact with people. He bumps into people. He reads the whole menu. He steps into line in the wrong place. He's not very good at these things and a guy tells him so.

Redfield watches life from a table off in the corner, nursing a complimentary coffee, peeking out at Juliet. As people walk by he matches them with movie stars. It's easier that way to keep them not real. He begins to think he sees some of the same people he saw in Connecticut or New Jersey, maybe Virginia. He has a real good glow. He begins to sweat. He needs a cool drink. He thinks they're all watching him. He thinks he's maybe been here before, but that can't be. Maybe he's read it all or heard it or saw it somewhere before. Juliet's in the shade. She's got postcards. She's writing. He wonders how long is a little bit.

He gets back in line, gets a cup, but can't find the soda pop. He follows the people in front of him, hoping they know how to do this.

"A small beverage," the cashier says. "That will be sixty cents."

"Where do I get my small beverage?"

"Over there, sir. Unlimited refills."

Like life, he thinks.

He says, "You mean if I come back here ten years from now, I can have one?"

"Excuse me, sir?"

"Nothing," Redfield says. He doesn't want to pester the guy. He worries about the interstate fast food security.

He gets his drink and sits back down. There's now a man and a woman at the table next to him. He's seen them before. The guy looks like Kojak. Redfield keeps looking at him. The guy looks back, then to his wife, and says something to her Redfield can't hear. The guy looks up again and says, "You got a problem, buddy?"

"Yeah," Redfield says. "You got an ugly dog."

The guy smiles.

"How do you know I got an ugly dog?"

"Guy like you would have an ugly dog."

"You're funny. He's funny, isn't he," the guy says to his wife.

"Now I know." Redfield says. "You're Marcia and Harry. I read it on your spare tire when I passed you back in Bristol, Tennessee. Where's your Winnebago? Where's your dog? I'm Redfield."

Redfield gets up, knocking over what's left of his small beverage, and they all shake hands.

"People look like they're enjoying themselves," he says, sweeping a hand toward the other people, women with walkers, tour-bus folks, locals, children. "Kind of like a fort on the old Chisholm Trail."

"Yes," Harry says. "It's a good day to travel. Where are you headed?"

"Just out and about. Where are you going?"

"We're going to my mother's in San Diego," Marcia says. "We've just been to Las Vegas."

"Well, have a nice trip," Redfield says, not knowing how to end what he started. He stands there until finally he gives off a smile and walks away.

He tells Juliet to hurry, they have to leave, and she doesn't ask why.

They ride in off high fault scarp, off the burnt humps of the San Gabriel Mountains, falling roads that scare you because there is so much to see. They cross the San Andreas Fault, the Sierra Madre Fault, the Whittier Fault, the Raymond Hill Fault, coming closer and closer to the Los Angeles Basin. Redfield drives at speed, aggressively scooting up the miles between lanes of stalled traffic, thinking always he'll be at the epicenter if and when the next buffeting comes. He knows that when the next big snap comes he doesn't want to be in this place with these people. He doesn't want to be in anybody's horror story except his own.

★

Redfield's father stayed in Burbank the spring and summer of 1948. He lived in a house on Santa Anita and it's still there, 235 Santa Anita. You can see it if you want. He tells Juliet he feels stones moving in his heart. He thinks about his old man. His thoughts are fast and generous. She tells him, My heart, too.

Up the street are the Verdugo Mountains, home of Griffith Observatory, Starlight Theatre, Wildwood Canyon, the Hollywood sign. The mountains dead-end the street, humping out of the earth so abruptly they could still be rising. The photos read: *Griffith Observatory Mt. Hollywood* and *February 18, 1948 at the beach—nice and warm.* He's squatting in front of the Griffith Observatory. Then, the Nash is parked nose to the ocean. The passenger door is open and he's sitting on the seat with foot on ground, smokes rolled up in shirtsleeve. And a third that says nothing. It's of him leaning on the Nash, license plate number 74X658. Behind him is the bungalow, 235 Santa Anita.

Redfield knocks on the door. A man answers, only speaks Spanish. Redfield smiles, tells his story and pauses. The man smiles back and says something. Redfield speaks again. The man speaks again. Neither of them knows what the other is saying, Redfield smiles and says goodbye. The man smiles and waves.

Juliet is sitting on the curb in her new leathers. She's flicking stones across the street into the storm drain.

"So?" she says.

"Well I really couldn't tell, but I think it was a boat guy. You know, a Vietnamese or a Cambodian."

"What'd he say?"

"Stuff those guys say. How the hell do I know? It was quite friendly or so it seemed. I think if we got to know him we'd like him. See, they'd do a little special on us and we'd maybe get on *60 Minutes* and then we'd become sound bits . . ."

Juliet isn't listening anymore. She's feeling the pain again. She can only liken it to contractions, or maybe it's like epileptic seizure or bad orgasm. She rummages around in her head trying to identify the pain as a step to gaining ascendancy over it.

"I gave my baby away like that famous woman in New Jersey." She flings pebbles to the drain, where they clatter and drop.

"It will get better."

"It will never get better. Did you say sound bits? What the fuck are sound bits?"

"Maybe we could go to Hollywood. Tell our story."

"Run to them. Yeah, like they're the big confessor. Life is getting to be so fucking public. You run to them and tell your story and they give absolution and reward. How perfect."

"What if they don't like your story?"

"Because it's been told, I guess. But this is *my* story. This is *my* fucking story."

"God loves all his children. All their stories."

She lets her body slump against his, her head tipped onto his shoulder.

"I think things I shouldn't," he says, "and I'm afraid my mind gets read."

Across the street, a woman comes onto her porch. She looks at them sitting on the curb. She's old enough to have been here when Redfield's father lived a summer in California. Maybe he dated the old bird. Maybe they went to the movies, went to see *Key Largo, Red River, Treasure of the Sierra Madre.* "The Streets of Loredo" was a hit single. The bikini showed up. Babe Ruth and Mahatma Gandhi died. Orville Wright died and Chucky broke the sound barrier in a rocket-powered Bell X-1 at thirty-five thousand feet. *Hamlet* won the Academy Award, posthumously, of course.

Redfield lets himself lie down gently on the concrete sidewalk and Juliet goes with him, her head on his shoulder. He adjusts his sunglasses and concentrates on his breathing. Something is slipping away and he isn't sure what it is. He's caught up with himself here, been out ahead, and now feels himself at his back.

"Last fall," he says, "this girl came up to me after class. It was around before Thanksgiving time. She wanted to have coffee. She was pretty to me and I liked that. So we were having coffee and she says she admires me, likes me for my maturity. Then she starts to cry. It was only a little bit of crying, but enough to make her face all wet. She tells me she needs my help. She's gone and gotten herself pregnant and wants to know if I'll take her to Harrisburg so she can get an abortion."

"Oh, Redfield. That poor girl."

"Her boyfriend was back home. She couldn't tell him. I asked her if she had any friends. She did but wanted to go with me, even though I was a stranger, because there was something about me she trusted. She planned on finishing her four years, and it being a small school, she didn't want word to get out. She didn't want this haunting her. She thought of me as someone who wouldn't be around very long."

"That was a shitty thing to say."

"No. I think she meant it as a compliment. Kind of an admiring thing."

"So what happened?"

"I took her to Harrisburg. They were protesting when we got there. There was a coffee shop where we were supposed to meet these people who'd escort us in. They formed up, four or five of them, to take us through. She held on to me inside the circle. We started out and they stopped us. They had posters and little wrinkled dolls and jars of stuff. I remember their faces. They all had Gumby mouths and little white faces. Chicken faces all around us, yelling. She had a hold of my arm so tight my hand was going numb."

Juliet moves even closer and gets her arm across his chest. She gets her head to his cheek so he can smell her hair, know she's there.

"One of the chicken faces reached through and jammed a little fetus doll between us. I grabbed his arm and dragged him inside the circle, then punched him in the head about three times. Opened up his nose. That got us moving again. Later, inside, the escorts told me they were nonviolent and they didn't like me for doing what I did. The police started showing up, so they sent me out the back door and told me to wait in the car."

Somewhere it starts to thunder. Redfield thinks it sounds like distant war, or is it war like the sound of distant thunder or is it just distant thunder? That's all he wants it to be. He now holds tightly to Juliet's arm locked across his chest.

"After the abortion we went back to my room and she stayed the night. My roommate was away. I held her and rubbed her back. Cold water gave her cramps, so I got her some soup. In the night she woke up. She was hot and sweaty, so I gave her a sponge bath. She was shaking like a leaf. In the morning she told me how easy it would be to fall in love with me. That's why she couldn't see me again. She wanted a career. Wanted to be a lawyer. Her boyfriend was a lawyer. Her whole family and his whole family were lawyers and falling in love with me would get in the way of that. Is this an extraordinary life?"

"How do you mean that?"

"How do I mean."

★

They ride into the Verdugoes, up and down through the stratas of smog. These hills must burn before they can seed themselves. They fight to burn. They come to depend on arsons.

L.A. is gray. L.A. is blue. L.A. is green. L.A. is yellow.

They can see the Hollywood sign. In the Hollywood hills they're shooting a movie. Redfield and Juliet stop to watch. The action is expression by expression, frame by frame, *richer, richer, richer.*

"It's not a movie," Juliet says. "I think it's a music video."

Cameras turn and poise, bob imperceptibly on steel necks, like dinosaur heads, massive and fluid. Cables. Silver mirrors, umbrellas and trailers, steel and aluminum rods all closing in on a few square feet of earth where currently nobody stands. This is what they see.

Redfield decides his father couldn't have stayed here because there was no room for him. No one really lives in these mountains anyway. No one comes here except scientists and killers and people who make movies. His father liked to hunt and fish and must've missed knowing where the deer and trout and partridge were. He didn't want to have to find them all over again. He lacked the nerve.

They ride to the Griffith Observatory and see the Tesla coil. The air goes full with high voltages of high-frequency alternating current. This was exciting in its time and still is for many who know about such stuff. Redfield is bored, wants away from the current, way away.

He finds Juliet outside. She's over the rail picking clusters of chaparral pea, the red lavender blossoms the only color against the dry hillsides.

"Time to go," he says.

She fills her pockets and climbs back over the rail.

"I'm ready," she says.

Up and down the boulevard alone in traffic, traffic, the tall leggy eucalyptus trees come from Australia. They are white in the sun, could have bone inside their skin. He sees knees and thighs and calves. He wants to dress them, wants to stroke them. He points them out to Juliet and she says they are quite beautiful, they don't belong here.

Late in the day he tires of his search, confesses he didn't know what he was looking for anyways. Whatever it was, it's paved over, it's part of the interstate mall system, the swarm and squirm of L.A. It just isn't a big deal anymore, and besides, he's broken a cardinal rule of the tour: avoid cities. He's relieved and disappointed. At a light he tells Juliet he has to see a man in Carson City.

On the way out of L.A. town, he hears every name in a song, sees every place in a movie, listens to old Johnny Carson and the smart-ass youngster comedians: *So this is my first time in L.A., I'm from Brooklyn. Did you ever notice all the cars? Beautiful downtown Burbank . . . love ya, baby, love ya.* He begins to lose his nerve, fears the edge that Asphalt gave him might be slipping. He passes cars, runs a red light, cuts off a little pickup and secures the fast lane. His eyes flee across all signs looking for the word *north*. His insides begin crawling up his neck.

"Free Rodney King," he yells. "Free Rodney King."

★

So at dusk they bank north, picking up the Pacific Coast Highway, wandering in just as it turns to night. Redfield is elated. He has always wanted to see California in the dark. His headlight catches the night eyes, herefords and horses, cats and foxes, raccoon and possum. No one else is on the road so he has both slim lanes, and the moon is bright.

They enter the steep cliffs and are drenched in mountain fog, fog so thick like live steam from a fresh boiler. It builds up on their leathers and skates with the wind. Redfield gets the most of it and for that he's happy.

Out there, off his left hand, is the Pacific Ocean, the cold California current. Whales: humpback, blue and minke, feeding on krill and schooling fish, bubbling, vocalizing.

A bumblebee thunks him in the head. He's running north. He's in flight. He's a moving shadow in the night season.

Out there in the air: Thayer's gull, the western gull, the least tern and maybe somewhere a magnificent frigate bird. Turnstones. Oyster catchers . . .

Out there in the water: sponges and hydroids, jellyfish, flatworms, mollusks, anthropods, echinoderms, stars, stars in the water. Brachiopods. Chordates . . .

Out there: hagfish, lampreys, rays and wrasses, skates, anchovies, coho, grunion, barracuda and tuna . . .

Out there: Japan and China and Afghanistan and Iran and Iraq and Syria and Egypt and Algeria and Morocco and the Atlantic Ocean and Norfolk, Virginia. Out there comes back to here, but out there isn't America. It's the vision of Balboa, tried for treason, beheaded.

Out there: two hundred miles more of the long American arm.

The road is a snake notched into the high mountains. He can't tell if the land has risen up or fallen away. Whatever it did, it's still doing it.

ROCK SLIDES, the sign says. Is that a warning or merely a law of physics. Maybe both. Maybe neither.

Yeah, he thinks. Rock does slide. It makes a wicked loud screaming noise. Some rocks roll and others tumble. Rock and roll. Rolling Rock. Rock slide. Juliet is feeling for his ribs. He was the one who screamed. It didn't come from the rocks.

He's loving how dark it gets at night. He feels as if he's driving *four hundred miles an hour.* His arms trill; they run with pit bulls wearing spiked collars, pit bulls dragging log chains. His arms are chrome and they're fused to the buckhorns. He can feel Juliet's hands hooking into his belt. Her Connecticut boyfriend, the father of her child, was New Age before New Age was New Age.

"Fuck him," Redfield yells to the wind. He's lucky there's a continent between me and him, the spineless puke. It's moments like this he comprehends discovery: fire, gold, gravity, electricity, the button, a little boy and his tweeter. He wonders how many nights he spent coming home from the bars. Not enough. What bent of mind values the intellectual over the corporeal?

This is my life and I am the designated driver.

★

Ten hours go by and daybreak finds them dozing in a garlic field somewhere near Hollister in the Great Basin, the foothills of the Diablos.

She wakes again to him sitting by her side. How many days has it been? Been since what? She can't remember bedding down for the night, but she's in her new leathers and she has a blanket over her. They're in a shady spot by a stream and the air is pungent with the smell of garlic.

She can feel her sweat trickling, dampening her body. She smiles because she has apprehended all of this: the garlic, the warm leather, her milky body, the trilling grasshoppers, before memories of her child brimmed over not a second ago.

He has a canteen. He wets a bandanna and washes her face. He's singing: *Oh little baby don't say a word, Mama's gonna buy you a mockingbird . . .*

"Where are we?"

"Somewhere near Hollister. Somewhere over the rainbow. This is where it all began."

"What do you mean?"

"You ask that a lot."

"So what do you mean?"

"This is where the Drunken Booze Fighters rioted in 'forty-seven. This is where they got the idea for the movie *The Wild One.* It's all in the book *Hells Angels* by Hunter S. Thompson, a true American, and if you want to see how it ends, you'll have to read the book."

"Oh, that's nice."

She strokes her leathers. She likes them. They make her feel smooth and quick, the length of her body, the skin over her bones. She wiggles her toes. He must've slipped her boots off. Ostrich Lady bought her those boots, insisted Juliet let her.

Ostrich Lady said: Every time you wear them you'll think of me.

Juliet said: Who are you people and why are you so nice?

Ostrich Lady said: You're silly. Just nice people and probably this way because our whole lives we couldn't afford to be otherwise.

"Are we still in California?"

The last thing she thinks she remembers is being in California at night, the landscape malevolent. She was afraid of being eaten alive by rock or ocean, so she put her arms around him, hooked her hands inside his belt and went into something like sleep.

"Not for long."

"Do we have to travel so quickly? We can't see anything."

"I see what I want to see."

"But you can't see anything."

"I see it the way I want to, like the pony express, like the 'forty-niners, like Chuck fucking Yeager. You know I have as much a responsibility *to be* seen."

"I think I know what you mean," she says.

"What do I mean?"

"It's an Einstein kind of thing. Like point of view, like westward expansion, like how you don't age when you travel at the speed of light, how the fuck do I know? Jesus, I'm starting to sound like you."

"Take a drink," he says, handing her the canteen.

She sits up and the water still runs down her chin. She

takes another mouthful, gargles and spits. She wants her toothbrush.

"You know that tooth-brushing can get to be a habit."

"You're crazy."

"You know, I was thinking. We'll go back down to Hollywood and sell your story. We'll tell them it's about a love child that gets given away, but because of the soundtrack, a job-training program and a more mature attitude, everyone is happy. It'll be a sisterhood thing, a gift of life."

"That's cruel."

"Hey, I know about this stuff. I have had seven months of economics, English, art history, religion, science, foreign policy, sociology, psychology and P.E. I read fifty books simultaneously, all the while keeping up with my leisure reading. I have made inroads into vocabulary. No silent fucking generation for me."

"Yeah, yeah, yeah. Big fucking whoop."

Redfield stands, waving his arms as if to gain flight. He lifts a boulder and throws it down. He picks up a branch and breaks it over the boulder. He winces and holds his ribs, goes down on his knees beside her, his brow tight, shiny with sweat.

"When the fuck are you boys going to grow up?"

"I am proof that a little knowledge goes a long way, like Amway products, like a pyramid scheme."

"You are proof that a little knowledge is dangerous, like—"

"Like what?"

She searches her mind for a dangerous knowledge. She wants to be smart and quick, full of sharp retort, but she can't.

"Like me, I guess."

Redfield lies down on the blanket. His breathing evens out. He thought he was getting better, but maybe not that much better.

"Then we'll sell my story," he says.

"What's your story?"

He thinks. He conjures up words, but none of them are his story. They only describe his story.

He says, "Just a guy on the road. That's all. Just a guy on the road."

Juliet looks down at her cousin. His eyes are red and puffy. Every movement he makes is tired, painful. He looks like something dying.

Maybe she could call their parents. Get picked up. They could fly out and save them, make it all better, but those days passed by not so long ago. It is so, that you can love someone to the point where you would die before you'd disappoint them, or at least stab out your eyes if you did.

She strokes his forehead. She doesn't know if he slept or not. She thinks, Asphalt must have lit his burner before they left. No matter. He's her cousin and what could be worse than what she's done?

"I'm afraid," he says, "that I'll grow up and be one of those old men who stares off, vacant, slow, mute. I won't have anything to talk about. I'll have a slow mind full of mistaken ideas. I won't have any words."

"Don't worry about that. This is where you live. Right here and right now, with me."

"I'm afraid of everything. I feel brittle. Don't blame me if I'm afraid of you. Afraid always. All the time. Afraid you won't like me."

Juliet is surprised by this. She thinks how strange it is, this way he feels about her. She doesn't say anything. She cups his face, here and there, moving her hand again and again.

"Poor Redfield," she says.

"I was going somewhere, but now I'm just traveling."

She thinks, What could be worse than what I've done? What I've done is *good*. I saved my baby from illegitimacy. Everybody has a right to be born legitimately. It's a gift of sisterhood. *Blah. Blah. Blah.* So why do I want to die or kill? Have already died and killed. Why is my mind this razor across my wrist?

She traces his lips with her fingers, lets them slide into his mouth. She leaves them there and lets him taste them, feels him sucking. She's afraid because she feels so sane.

Redfield lets off the throttle and pulls in the clutch. The big twin cylinders are silent coasting, dropping out of the Sierras, and abruptly the world goes quiet, something like flying as they land on the deck of Nevada, on the coast of the Great Basin.

Last fall, Redfield drove north to visit home. It was only a five-hour run from southern Pennsylvania to upstate New York. He arrived in the evening. His mother was at the house in town. She told him his father was out to the farm and that surprised him because he knew how much his father hated it. Redfield crossed the Seneca and made his way down River Road. There was a wooden FOR SALE sign planted in the front yard. It wouldn't be long before there'd be a dusting of snow. Already the air was laden with the smells of silage and cold woodsmoke from last night's fires. He'd come north for reasons he couldn't remember. Maybe to simply not go back. Maybe to apologize for something. Maybe just to see his mother and father, just to see the farm. He hadn't figured on seeing this FOR SALE sign.

He went into the barn for his chainsaw. He took time to sharpen it, to flush out the tank and refill it. By now his father had come to the front porch. He was wearing a kind of turban, probably a headgear he'd fashioned to hold ice. He stood with his hands clasped in front of him. They nodded to formally acknowledge each other, then Redfield topped the sign in one-foot increments all the way to the ground. His father still stood quietly. He got a can of gas and doused the sign pieces, then torched them. *Woof,* a ball of fire sucking air shot high and disappeared, leaving more quiet flames to consume the wood. He waved to his father and his father waved back. They even would have smiled at each other if smiling were normal between them, because this wasn't about anger or destruction. It was about signs.

Redfield got on the bike and made the five-hour haul back into the Commonwealth of Pennsylvania, feeling something near to peace for a while.

★

They've made the run across California and into the Sierras. Outside Sacramento they tied in with twenty bikers and rode with them until they all dropped off for Yosemite. Sacramento was the western terminus for the pony express. Redfield and Juliet kept on climbing east.

To the right and left they watched and rode the gradual incline to the Truckee Pass. Heavy snows can come in September. The soils are shallow. The rocks here formed slowly, cooling from their molten states. At Donner Pass, the flow lines are well delineated. And that's why the people came in '49. This rock is deep-seated, dense and strong, a host for ore.

They drop south and skirt Lake Tahoe for twenty miles. The lake sparkles like a jewel at six thousand feet.

"Like a jewel, like a jewel," Redfield says to the wind.

They know they're in Nevada when a highway patrolman stops them and asks for identification and then gives them a summons because they don't have their helmets on.

"Thank you, thank you," Redfield says. "You've probably saved our shabby lives."

"Don't be a smartass, Redfield," Juliet says.

"Don't be a smartass, Romeo," the trooper says. "Hey, I didn't get it at first. You're Romeo and Juliet."

"Yeah, you probably thought we were dead," Redfield says.

Now the trooper is laughing. He can't wait to tell someone, tell the guys back at the barracks, tell his wife.

"Well, we didn't die. We faked it and we've been hiding out in America. We aren't even Italian. We faked

that, too, Hey, do you know an old-timer in the Tennessee Highway Patrol, guy named Johnny Dupree?"

"No I don't."

"Guy I know."

"Redfield," Juliet says. "Be nice to the man. He's just
doing his job."

So now they're in Nevada, a state of chance, a state
where kids who listen to Judas Priest kill themselves,
where sagebrush is a flower, where the telephone pole is
a tree.

Late in the day they find Raymond Landers on the
outskirts of Carson City. He has a house in a new devel-
opment on the edge of town. He's just getting in himself.
He was down to a fireman's barbecue in June Lake,
where he used live. Clint Eastwood was there. Clint's a
friend of the June Lake Volunteers. During the filming of
High Plains Drifter, the park service insisted that fire trucks
be on the site so the June Lake Volunteers were hired.

Raymond's wife died in 1982 and now he spends most
of his time with Christina, a nurse, and some of his time
with his good friend Teddy, who's retired.

They all sit out on the patio. Teddy is from Burbank.
He tells Redfield that after World War II, it was as if the
country was suspended; men and women who worked
in factories sixty to seventy hours a week were all of a
sudden laid off. He says, The army was laying them off
too, if you know what I mean. Everything seemed to
stop. Burbank was beautiful back then. Orchards and
farms. It was a farm town.

"Your mom called," Raymond says. "She asked if you

came this way if I could make sure you're all right. Christ, I haven't talked to that woman in fifteen years. Your father wouldn't talk. I don't know what in hell his problem is. You left school, she said."

"No big thing. Look at it this way. There's a lot of schools I *haven't* flunked out of yet."

Raymond Landers walks the patio, shaking his head. He gets near where Redfield is sitting and looks at him. He shakes his head again, thoughts go by his brain, they come in and out of mind. He drags Redfield up out of his chair and puts his arms around him. He holds him tightly, hugging him stiffly, clapping him on the back.

This is a reunion. Raymond Landers's eyes go to water. The skin on his face is thin, the capillaries close to air. This is a reunion not lost on all those present. It's a man and the son of his best friend, a long time lost.

Raymond Landers sits him down and tells how he went back East for a while but couldn't take it so he made the dash again to California. He talks quickly, filling in the years. He got a job with Standard Oil and worked his way up to manager of the station at Third and Vermont. All the stars came there for gas—Sammy Davis, Jerry Lewis, Nanette Fabray, Marlon Brando. Randolph Scott was a true gentleman, and Clark Gable would have them put his rig on the lift so he could change his own oil. Jerry Lewis was a whiz, Nanette Fabray was a stunner, Sammy Davis was a real talent and Brando had a '55 port-hole T-bird.

Redfield watches Raymond Landers. His eyes roll like

his father's and his laugh, the way it starts to come and gets lost inside his face and shakes down through his body.

Redfield keeps watching Raymond Landers. He tries to realize he's here in Carson City with his father's old friend. He keeps getting closer to the moment, to being in the moment, but then thoughts of coming and going take over. Here he feels known, he feels like there's stuff he has to learn, has to ask, has to find out. He thinks again about leaving immediately, but that wouldn't be polite.

He asks him about the trip in '48. Raymond says, Wait a minute, and goes inside for a *Rand McNally Road Atlas.* They stare at the country, flip to the eastern states and come west. Each map, the names of places spring his memory to reveal the names of people, what they did, where they've been.

. . . In Tucumcari they hit a whiteout, a blizzard so fierce they couldn't tell up from down. Ahead they could see the mere shadow of lights off in the desert. It was an old couple who'd been following the power lines for their bearings, but the road curved and the lines kept straight. The car wrecked. The husband had a finger amputated earlier in the day. They made room for the old couple in the Nash. Tucumcari was home of Billy the Kid.

"Why did my father go?"

"What the hell was Jimmy going to do back there, anyways? His parents were much older. You probably don't even even remember them. Your grandfather brewed his own beer and worked for two dollars an hour. Where was he going to go? Barrel factory? Box factory? Shoe factory? We always worked in those days. Emmett's lunch. Sprague and Carleton. Post office. Ellis Hotel. Now that was fun, the Ellis Hotel. There were no bars, but you could go to a hotel and get a room and order room service. Let me tell you, there were some good parties, some that shouldn't oughta been."

He stares at the maps of the country as if they are photographs and the atlas is an album. Maps: the history of a country. Maps of America: history and bible.

"Know something?" Teddy says. "In Russia they don't have any accurate maps. No good ones, and that's no shit. The country has been run over so many times and every time the enemy came in they'd use a Russian map, so the Russians purposely print phony maps. You can't go anywhere in the country because you never know where you are."

"How do you know that?" Raymond Landers says.

"I know it because I read it."

But Raymond Landers isn't listening. He says, "The year we were out here, your dad worked on the docks at Freuhoff Trucking and I worked in a stove factory running forklift. We joined a group for young people at the Catholic church and they'd have parties. We had a good time that summer. We used to go tuna fishing in Ensenada. We went with a guy named Jack Pharr and some of his buddies from Northrup. Jack designed the prototype for the Stealth, the original flying wing."

Redfield pulls out a photo of his father with a yellow-tail. It says: *May 28, 1948 Fishing trip to Ensenada, Mexico 60 lb. Tuna.* His father is holding up a fish and smiling.

"Christina," Raymond says. "Come look at this. Who says I can't catch fish? Christina doesn't think I can catch fish."

"Why'd he leave?" Redfield says. "Why'd he go back home?"

"Oh your dad, he had a little honey back home waiting. He wanted to be with her. The twin sister to this girl's mother," he says, pointing to Juliet. "We were sweet, you know. I could've been your father. And, darling, you are just as beautiful as your mother and her sister."

Raymond Landers shoots Juliet a killer smile and pats the back of her hand. She's been composing postcards in her head: *Thought I'd let you know where I am in the world . . . Uplifted and dropped down in a kind of foreign world once again . . . Have met up with lots of people . . . How are you? Thinking of you. Where are you?*

"We got mixed up with some señoritas down there in old Mexico. Cost us ninety dollars for shots to get un-mixed up. We were sick for days. I'll tell you, we were a bunch of chowderheads. We didn't know shit."

And now they all realize they are here in this geometry of connections, lines oblique, tangential, parallel. What am I to you? What are you to me? Who is blood? Who is friend? Who is friend of blood? Who am I to me?

It's another patio in Nevada, opening and looking east. It's another patio with roof, picnic table, wooden furniture, fat cushions and a barbecue. Redfield moves to take out his knife to pare his nails. Juliet feels her milk dampening her shirt.

"He had a little honey he had to go home to. They got married in a little church on Lake Winnipesaukee in New Hampshire. That's where your mothers are from."

"You want a little nip in that?" Teddy says to Redfield.

"Yeah, I'll take a little nip."

"Me too," says Teddy.

Raymond goes inside for a bottle of Kahlúa.

Great shadows begin to descend, shadows like the tide, like banks of drifting snow. Lights pin the sky and mountains. Redfield says a prayer for cold. He wants to need a blanket to stay warm tonight.

"Redfield," Juliet says. "When I flew out here there were these older women sitting side by side. They were triplets. They wore the same white nylon windbreakers. Their hair stood out from their heads. They had perms that made them look like they had big heads. They took time to be triplets. Clothes, hair, makeup, thick, thick tans. They made the same facial expressions in triplicate. I guess it's easy. We were going through O'Hare. That's why they were on the plane. They were skinny, pretty women with similar mouths. No, they were lipless, like reptiles."

"Three hipless women," Redfield says.

"They were scaring me and then I thought it was a sign. I was going to have twins or triplets. I started throwing up after that."

"Juliet, you're remembering stuff."

"What's the matter with your memory, honey?" Christina says.

"Nothing," Juliet says, waving her hand and smiling. "It's just a little joke between us."

"Juliet, you were remembering."

"No I wasn't. I won't. I can't. Forget it."

*

That night they lie across from each other in a travel-trailer camper Raymond Landers has parked by the garage. They lie tucked away in small beds. The night is cold. They're in the high desert.

"I like him a lot," Redfield says. "He's the kind of guy who always keeps a hundred-dollar bill hidden in his wallet, from even himself."

"Yes, they're nice people. We've only met nice people since we've been on our trip."

"I have this yearning, this twenty-three-year-old yearning. I'm starting to enjoy life. Things seem to be beginning again. I'm feeling better."

"I'm happy you've found what you're looking for. I'm really happy for you."

He can hear her turning in the bed, turning her back to him.

"Is something wrong, I mean aside from the obvious."

"Go to sleep, Redfield."

"You know, I was thinking. Maybe we could trade the bike in and get one of these motorhomes. Get something twenty-five, thirty feet. AC, generator, microwave, bath, big Chevy engine, sleeps four or five people. Icebox. LP gas. I wonder if they come with a washer-dryer."

He can hear her turning his way again.

"And who would those people be?"

"What people?"

"The four or five people."

"I don't know. Just people."

"But there's just you and me, Redfield, remember? We're the only people in the world, so go to fucking sleep. Please."

It isn't too hard to figure out that Juliet isn't as happy as she claimed. It isn't hard to figure that out, even for Redfield. He'll have to do something to cheer her up.

"Juliet, he was on the trip with my father back in 1948. That's over forty years ago."

But she doesn't say anything. She's understanding that no matter how hard she tries, the pain will always be with her. Once she had a baby and now she doesn't. It's that simple. She pretends to be asleep and he pretends to believe her.

Redfield thinks about home, thinks about his mother and father. He remembers the last night they spent together before he left for school. Earlier that day he'd sold his cattle and said goodbye to the neighbors. His mother cooked a pot roast and they had a quiet dinner together.

At midnight, he was in the kitchen when he heard his father get out of bed. He was having one of his headaches. He walked into the kitchen clutching his skull. Years ago he thought they were migraines, but they're different. He opened the cabinet door and went for the Old Grand-Dad, but it wasn't there. From the pantry he got a warm Falstaff. He held his head and drank while telling Redfield a story about a man who gets drunk and loses his watch and must get drunk again to find it.

The headaches had been coming mostly at night, five a day for two or three weeks. His eyelids were swollen and drooped. It was a steady, boring, burning pain. Twice he'd torn the bedroom door off the hinges.

"They call them suicide headaches because that's how some people solve the problem," he said.

Redfield didn't say anything. He stood with his back to the sink, watching. He could see another surge of pain begin to build in his father's head. They'd argued at dinner again about selling, and Redfield couldn't help but feel a little responsible for his father's pain.

Blue light came from the living room, the sound of the television. Redfield's mother was watching a tape of the Boston Pops. She thinks he gets the headaches because of stress and because he had to sleep in a hamburger when he went to hamburger school to secure his first franchise. He wanted to be an artist, but instead he ended up with a fast-food franchise in Auburn, New York, and then another one. He was conscientious, persevering, resourceful and driven. He was talented at doing something he hated.

He used to hire kids, but then the kids didn't want to work anymore so he hired old people, the oldest he could find. He liked the old people. They needed the money to live, not to buy music or jeans or hundred-dollar sneakers. They couldn't be corrupted into thinking that what they were doing was important. They knew it was just a job, not a way of life. They knew enough to wash their hands.

His father stood up and went to the kitchen door where by the casing there was a patch of clear warm wall. Redfield knew what was coming. He could have stopped him, but he didn't. His father began to beat his head against the wall. He pounded away until the wall went red with his blood and by then he'd knocked himself out and he slumped to the floor.

He was only out for a moment, revived by his wife's cool fingers and an ice pack Redfield kept balanced on his head.

"Is your headache gone?" she whispered.

"Yes. I kind of miss it."

"Why don't you take a few days and go out to the farm? We do still own it."

She sat on the floor beside his head. He stared straight up at the ceiling.

"The farm," he said.

"You already miss Raymond, don't you? And he hasn't even gone."

"Raymond?"

Redfield went to the freezer for ice. It was moments like this that taught him there was more between his parents than just him. As he had come into their lives, he would soon move along to be on his own, and that night the lesson was singular and clear. He was their son, a visitor, always welcome.

She strokes his ruddy face. He wore deep furrows in his brow, deep folds between his nose and mouth.

"I saw in the news magazine," she said, "that nice Dr. Overholt died. He's the one who operated on Raymond's chest when he was a little boy. Did you know he was one of the very first to make a link between smoking and lung cancer? I didn't know that. Did you?"

"No."

"Why don't you go out to the farm for a few days. You know how much you like to be alone."

He didn't say anything. He must have been thinking about the flashing lights that went off in his head, trying to remember them but not being able to. He knew he'd recognize them when he saw them again.

When he first bought the farm it was an investment. The land fell to the Seneca, where there was a boat landing. And higher up, across the road, was a house and a barn and acres facing south where he and Redfield planted Christmas trees, Scotch pine and balsam. He used to get a big kick out of going to the farm. He liked to put on a pair of boots and find cowshit to walk in. He'd get projects in his head. He'd get hedge trimmers and flail away at the lilacs until he got stung and then he'd get a badminton raquet and start swatting hornets. Afternoons he'd sit around in his Bermuda shorts with no underwear on, listening to Paul Harvey on the radio, yelling at him, cussing him out.

He admired his son for moving in, admired him for doing a man's work.

But this land had a high line running through it and the Christmas trees grew around the towers. Every year there'd be a buzzing in his ears and it got louder and louder. He stopped going and didn't see his son so much because Raymond never came into town.

It wasn't just buzzing, though. He was hearing voices like on a radio. Then the headaches started and he started talking about selling.

She was singing to him. She was stroking his head and singing a song about time.

"Look," he said, fishing a newspaper clipping out of his breast pocket.

She took it from him and read how in Gayford, Minnesota, a jury awarded farmers a million dollars because stray electrical current cut milk production. The Northern States Power Company had failed to warn farmers about errant electricity entering the ground from grounded electrical distribution systems.

She refolded the clipping and handed it to him, shaking her head and making a *tsk* sound with her mouth.

"You just don't get it, do you?" he said.

"Get what?"

"This electromagnetic radiation. It causes insomnia, mood swings, fatigue, cancer, miscarriage, birth defects, brain tumors, headaches. It's all around us: the television, lights, digital clocks, microwaves, electric blankets. Promise me we'll get rid of this stuff in the morning. Promise me you'll never sleep under an electrical blanket."

"I promise, dear. I promise," she said, now stroking his head more quickly, her touch a flutter.

"There's too much ugliness in this world. I'm not supposed to be here. We're not supposed to be here."

Redfield wanted to say, But we are here. I am here. Why can't we figure this out? But he didn't say anything. He stood there holding the ice tray in his hands all that time and had long since passed over to where the cold begins to burn.

"We'll sell the farm and be done with it. We'll find another one."

"How can I sell it, knowing what it can do to someone else? How can I do that to someone?" he said.

"You can't dear, you can't."

★

"Juliet," he whispers.

"What?"

"Just checking."

14

In the morning Raymond Landers takes Redfield for a tour, and Teddy goes along too. Juliet has found sleep and wants its harbor for as long as it will have her. She tells him to go ahead, she'll doze as long as she can. She tells him, Buy some postcards. She says it like, Don't forget to stop for milk, or, We need a loaf of bread. He tells her, yes, he will.

Raymond wants to show him Silver City, Virginia City, all the places from *Bonanza*.

"I miss the East a little bit," Raymond says. "I remember we used to go horned-pout fishing. We'd pay a farmer two bits to use his boat. We'd get brewed up and spiked in the back by them horns. I'm telling you, that was fun. Your dad, he was smart's a whip. A whiz. He had the touch."

"Why did he write *Boulder Dam* on the back of one of these pictures when he should have known the name was changed by 1948?"

"I don't know. How should I know stuff like that?"

"Look. There's the whorehouse," Teddy says.

They pass by a set of low buildings surrounded by a high steel wire fence. The seats in the car are soft leather. Redfield can't get away from the pain in his torso. He keeps sinking into it.

"They have really beautiful women in there. Young women, smart women. I met one downtown one night. She was making money to pay off her ranch in Montana. She was a barrel racer."

"I've known a few," Teddy says. "Fine girls. Real class. Good girls, too. Clean girls. What'd you think of the Dam, anyways?"

"Pretty impressive."

"Fucking dam," Teddy says. "Fucking Imperial Valley. God didn't mean for men to grow tomatoes in the desert. We'll pay for that dam on a grand scale."

Raymond insists that Redfield buy another canteen for the trip across the desert. He won't take no for an answer. He stops at a sporting goods store, goes in and buys it himself.

They stay out all day, eating greasy hamburgers and

drinking pitchers of beer. Redfield blows twenty bucks on slots and Teddy and Raymond laugh at him, tell him not to worry, he's cured, he'll never do it again. They thank him for the contribution to the Nevada treasury and each secretly slips him a twenty-dollar bill, making it very clear he's not to tell the other.

When they get back to the house, Christina turns the hose on them and Juliet hands out towels. She's had a good day. She slept and she ate big helpings of scrambled eggs and toast and, shortly after that, soup and crackers. She kept apologizing for sleeping so long, for eating so much.

It was easy for Christina to know that Juliet was caught up in something, but she didn't ask. Instead she cooked for her and talked, told her how she grew up in Colorado, had a horse she rode to school. She became a nurse and never married.

Juliet told her about her own horse. When she was in graduate school in upstate New York, she boarded the horse at Redfield's farm. He lived there all alone and she'd drive out to ride, to visit him. She always felt the pain in his life that he seemed unable to feel. Then she graduated and sold the horse. The two women spoke about missing their horses and that's where they came to understand each other.

That night they eat late, steaks on the grill.

Raymond Landers says he can't remember the last time he saw Redfield's father. He can't remember the last time he saw Redfield. It makes him sad.

"I remember when he was a baby," Juliet says. "He had a mop of curly black hair. When I first saw him, I thought he was a puppy. At least that's what I'm told."

Juliet pokes him with her toe and they all laugh.

Juliet whispers to Redfield, "I told Christina she was very beautiful, and you know what she said? She said beauty is a decision we all make. Isn't that wise?"

Redfield nods his head. "Yes it is," he whispers. "Yes it is."

She remembers the last Christmas at the farm. It was when life started changing. This memory she tries to stop, but she can't. It was Christmas before she finished graduate school, the last time she saw Redfield. Their two families came together at the farm in Conquest in New York.

Her mother and father had driven up from Connecticut with her graduation present, a '66 Corvette. It was the warmest Christmas on record and she and Redfield drove the north country in the light before dinner with the top down. They took a case of Champagne and stopped to see old friends of his in all the little towns, Victory, Red Creek, Butler, Rose, Cato, Savannah, Meridian, Montezuma, towns with names like cheap wine.

They sat in steamy trailers, cold and drafty houses, apartments over garages, in milkhouses. They talked about the price of heifers and hay, about the time they kicked the shit out of Weedsport in football, and they all thought she was his girlfriend from the city.

The weather turned cold on the way home, but they

didn't stop to put the top up. They only drove faster, anticipating the warmth of the wood stove. Dinner was waiting when they got there. Their mothers were hugging in the kitchen, spilling sherry down each other's backs. Living apart the way they did made a pain that quietly consumed them.

That night after everyone else had disappeared into the upstairs rooms, Redfield and Juliet, a little drunk, let their flannel shirts off their shoulders and rubbed each other's chest and back with Vicks. Juliet gave him his Christmas presents, a set of black leather boot chains and a lockback knife, some things every boy should have. He was sad and angry because he didn't think to have something for her. She laughed and told him, of course, don't be silly.

He went to the closet and took his letter jacket off the hook. He gave it to her, and she knew better than to refuse. She always had a kind of love for him, ever since he was a boy and wanted to be a farrier, hoof trimmer, cowboy, short order cook, New York Giant, hell on wheels, disaster in the making, a storm brewing.

In the morning for breakfast, she mixed Bloody Marys and Redfield made eggs and salsa. He called it his secret recipe, Salsa Juliet. They kept bumping into each other, flirting, and she had a fancy he was her boyfriend.

It was a beautiful morning. It'd snowed in the night and now the sun was coming off the fields, sending cannons of light through the windows. When he was finished eating, Redfield's father pushed back his chair and stood up. He tapped at his water glass with a spoon, like at a wedding when everyone wants the bride and groom to kiss.

It was then he told Redfield he was going to college, told Redfield he was going to sell the farm.

He said, "I'm going to sell this farm," and his voice was no more than a whisper. "It is possible for you to go to college and I'm asking you to trust me Raymond, please."

She knew it was the *Raymond, please* in his voice that sent Redfield to college in Pennsylvania.

She went on to graduate in the spring and took up with a guy she now wants to hate more than any other human being in the world, if for no other reason than he took Redfield's letter jacket when he left, something she'll never be able to tell Redfield. And that's his history. That's her history.

Redfield gets up, asks to use the phone. He's decided he wants to call home.

She wants to say no, doesn't know why.

"No," she says.

"What?" Christina asks.

"No," Juliet says. "I think I've had enough."

Redfield goes inside and calls home.

"Hey, Ma," he says. "It's me, Raymond. Guess where I am."

"I know where you are, dear. You're in Nevada. Raymond Landers called to say you got in. He said Juliet was with you. That's wonderful. Is that poor girl okay?"

"Yes, she is. I'm with her. Is my father there?"

"He's in the hospital, dear. Exhaustion and stress, but he's okay. Just a day or two. He's tired, you know. Don't say anything to upset Raymond."

Redfield feels a chill. He hunches his shoulders into his neck.

"You don't worry," she says. "You just do your little thing and we'll see you when you get home. I'll let them know Juliet is fine."

Redfield's mother hangs up. It's the way she is on the phone.

★

That night after Juliet has fallen asleep, Redfield goes out to change his oil. They'll be leaving in the morning, to where he doesn't know, but it's always good to change your oil.

Redfield can see the ember of a cigar. Teddy is sitting in a lawn chair in front of the garage door.

"Good evening," Redfield says.

"Good evening to you, young fella."

Redfield stands beside him, shuffling his feet, shifting his weight. The chrome catches moon and stars. It holds the light and gives it back, all at the same time.

"I used to ride," Teddy says. "Back in the fifties. I had one of them cycle bikes, a 1949 Norton 500 Iron International. It was smoke, let me tell you."

"That'd be worth some big money these days," Redfield says, feeling like it was all he knew to say.

"You're telling me. It almost cost me my life. I guess that'd be big money. Currently it's a pile of rust somewhere."

"How so?"

"I was running out to Barstow when my rear tire dropped off the berm. I tried to get it back up, but it wouldn't come. I was clocking for a telephone pole. To this day I don't know how I made it. I got all stove up. Bike went ass over tea kettle. Some weeks later when I got back on my feet I went out there and you know what I saw?"

"What?"

"Drilled right into that telephone pole was the earstem off my glasses."

"Jesus," Redfield says. "You're a lucky boy."

"Oh we had some fun back then, I'll tell you. Hey, do you mind if I change your oil? You've been some miles and you're tired, no doubt. I haven't had my hand on a wrench in a long time. Haven't fixed anything in a long time."

Teddy says the word *fixed* as if it has two syllables.

"Yeah, go ahead. I'll just sit right here and keep you company."

They raise up the garage door and wheel the bike close to the opening. The yard light and the garage light are sufficient, but Teddy insists on running a trouble light too. They find a tarp, a plastic tub and a pile of rags.

While Teddy works on the bike, Redfield wanders. He pokes around. The tools are hung by size. The bench tools, band saw, table saw, lathe are clean and draped with dustcloths. A generator. A ladder. Redfield finds a can of PVC cement. He shakes it, then unscrews the cap and holds the can to his nose. He breathes the fumes deeply, three, four, five times. A small explosion goes off in his head. Just a hardware junkie, he says to himself, and caps the can.

In the morning Juliet isn't speaking. It's cold. The mountains to the east are just taking light, their west slopes still black and blue, just starting to show their hardscrabble faces.

Raymond Landers is the only one awake to see them off. He kicks at the raked sand in his front yard, tells them he hates grass, tells them they're welcome to stay. Then he tells Redfield something.

He says, "Your father saved my life on that trip, you know. It was in Needles, California. We had a pretty good jag on when we went to sleep in this little motel. Well, he had to get up in the night and take a piss. He was sicker than a dog. Finally, he figured out it was the gas heater. It was unvented. He came in and dragged me out. We were both sick for a long time."

The sky is starting to bruise purple, brick red, lavender, slate gray. Redfield likes the story about how his father saved someone's life. But then again, what was he going to do? Not go back in? No matter. Every boy likes to know his father saved a life.

"Now, you two stay on the main roads. Be wary of strangers. Don't get caught out there alone or broke down or at night. There's a lot of strange things that happen out there."

He checks the canteens and says it again, Be careful.

Juliet doesn't want to leave this place where she's found sleep, but if they must, she hopes they die on the road.

The rimrock glows up with the skip of sunlight. Now the sky is royal; this blue is cobalt. Feel the heat walking the land, palming the sagebrush, its silvery cast from the light in its coat of soft hairs. Wandering over the grasses and forks, the greasewood, saltbush, rabbit brush, bitter-bush.

Then they're on their way, hard on a five-hundred-mile run through the high desert, riding out of the Humbolt Sink on the river's bitter, sinuous course. Sagebrush, cheatgrass, piñon pine, the silence left by a passing eigh-teen-wheeler. They're on this run through the Great Empty, breathtaking for what isn't there.

Out here there is only you and nature, you and land, water and atmosphere. Out here it is immediate and you are always alone because nature doesn't give a fuck about you. You think if it had wants it would want to be left alone, it would want to not want. So you apologize and pass through quickly, quietly and gently.

"I'm sorry," Redfield says.

I'm so sorry, Juliet thinks.

He already can feel a tiredness creeping up on him. It comes minute by minute, taking him under. It's like going into water. Slow in the shallows and driving strength in the current. It distracts him from small things. Like remembering to let out the clutch or to pull out in time with speed or that he needs to get gas. Combinations to locks. Once he's under that water it ices over. He can still breathe, but in the back of his head is the idea that he shouldn't be able to and maybe at any second he won't be able to.

He needs to shock himself out of it. The thought of a woman in a miniskirt and a bottle of Johnnie Walker. That helps. Gives a jog. The thought of something hard and fast for a night. The expanse of a woman's thighs when she crosses her legs. His father in the hospital. His home. Juliet.

When we were children, he remembers, we used to go up to Schroon Lake, where the families had a summer cottage. Me and Juliet and the twin mothers and the fathers. They'd cut us loose because we could both swim. One time I smashed my thumb but good. The nail went huge and black. So I took a three-eighths-inch drill with a finish nail for a bit and drilled through. It got hot and started to smoke. When I pulled away an arc of blood spurted, then died. Afterwards, she said my thumb looked like a picture of Jesus Christ. Yeah, a thumbnail sketch, I said, but I couldn't see it.

We had another thing we'd do where we'd melt crayons onto our skin where we had fine white hairs. We'd color our whole arms and then we'd peel it off. It always hurt her. She'd get teary-eyed, but she wouldn't let me stop. We sure used to have some fun.

In Winnemucca they stop to tank up and Redfield buys a map. Routes are no big deal in Nevada. They all run east-west, in and out, and to the north and south the land is corrugated by 128 mountain ranges.

This map has advertisements for motels, camp-grounds, casinos and missing children. The children's faces are amongst the ads for Bally's of Reno, Felton's Motor Inn, and one for a guy named Adolf V. Stankus, Jr., who'll buy your used military vehicles. He wants tanks and half-tracks. He'll take cannons in any condition.

Redfield and Juliet decide they are tired. They want to lie down and go to sleep. They wheel the bike around to the shade side. Juliet can't get these missing children out of her head. Every time she sees them, she sees her own infant. Every time Redfield sees them, he sees himself.

It's like that. Unmercifully, one after the other. They want to keep this map just a map, but they know they can't. You can't look at a map to gain scale or projection. The world is only in front of you, a long road sewn to your wheels. Redfield thinks how his father is the only man he knows who truly loves to be alone. Redfield gets a coffee, goes into the men's room and dusts it with crank, just a little bit. Something to jolt his brain, give it a slam.

Beyond Battle Mountain, in the Shoshone territory, there's an overturned U-Haul truck, a wrecker and two cars.

It's a big family and they're moving their belongings

out into the desert, tables and chairs and dressers, parts of beds. Everything is okay. They're waiting for another truck. They're headed for California. Redfield leaves them a canteen, then he and Juliet continue on, running over the Great Salt Lake Basin, the dry ocean floor of wave-cut benches, beaches, spits and bars.

It's 118 degrees, the air stinks with saltwater, night is coming and Redfield's nose bleeds slowly into his mouth.

On the wind they can smell Salt Lake. Redfield thinks
he wet his pants some time ago, but isn't sure. They're
dry now, stained black. He's back on the road, been on
it for a day, Juliet holding him in her arms. Most of
what's left behind is left behind. Out on the road you
don't need what's left behind, unless you need it.

Redfield's father and Raymond Landers hitched
through here on their way back East. They hit Salt Lake
at one in the morning, rumbling in on a bobtail headed
north to Montana. Two cops tried to shake them down,
but they wouldn't give in. They insisted on being taken

to the precinct, taken to a judge, put in jail, anything but pay off a bad cop. The cops let them go. They hitched a ride to Rock Springs, Wyoming, where they wanted to hop a freight but were warned off by a hobo, who told them there'd been a murder the night before, a woman killed by a vagrant and the bulls were working over everyone.

They had an offer to go north. A big tunnel job was opening up in Evanston, the Southern Pacific Railroad. Big tunnel. Big money. Raymond wanted to go, but Redfield's dad wanted to get home. So they took a bus to Chicago, they bummed a ride to Windsor Locks, Ontario, reentered at Niagara Falls and caught another bus across New York State. Redfield's father was one month shy of twenty and must've felt like he was coming off of something. He was. The biggest adventure of his young life. Getting away with his life. He'd seen California.

Redfield and Juliet make the run into the Wasatch, up through the black draws that descend on Salt Lake City. After L.A., they won't dally again in a city. Engine sound trumpets off the walls of Parley's Canyon, power in his hand. The higher he goes, the cooler it gets, the higher he wants to go.

At times there is no sun as the near stone walls rise hundreds of feet above their heads.

They enter the Untas in the late day, drop off the highway to look for shelter.

In Heber City they stop for the night at the Swiss Alps Inn. Across the street is Chick's and that's where they go for supper. Six bucks gets you chicken fried steak, green salad, mashed potatoes, mixed vegetables, a scone as big as your fist and a soda pop. Their waitress is all of sixteen and blond. Her name is Janet. After she leaves, Juliet says, "You know, if you were a star, they'd pay you to drink Pepsi."

"If I were a star, I wouldn't be drinking Pepsi."

"What would you drink?"

"Water, air, sunlight."

"You already do."

"Yeah, but it'd taste better."

"Oh, Redfield. You say the cutest things."

"Fuck off," he says, grateful she's speaking again.

When Janet comes back with their food, she wants to know where they have been and where they are going. It's what everyone has wanted to know, every pump jockey, fry cook, cashier and waitress. The big Harley, laden with gear, canteen, bedrolls, helmets, knapsack, bandannas snapping behind like pennants. Them in leather and sunglasses, a roadside attraction, something happening.

Redfield wants to tell her of his high intent, of running a ghost to ground, but the words don't come. He falls back on a recitation of place names, states, rivers and mountains.

She smiles, shakes her head and, even at sixteen, does one of those things women can do with their eyes.

Juliet smiles for the first time all day. By intent, she hasn't spoken much since Carson City. Now she's feeling a little better. She's coming to know some things about her haunted life.

"I would love to do that," Janet says.

Redfield thinks how he would love to do that, too.

"Are you married?" Janet says.

Before Redfield can answer, Juliet tells her they are married and headed for New Mexico.

"That's so sweet. You enjoy your dinner now, and if you need me just call."

"Why did you say that?" Redfield asks.

"It's Utah," Juliet says. "All the young girls are looking for someone to marry, to take them out of here. Don't you know this stuff? I didn't want her to think she had a chance and then be disappointed."

"But she does have a chance. I kind of like her bones."

"Oh, please. Don't be that way."

"At least you're talking."

"I'm better now."

"I'm happy for you."

"I had a memory in Carson City. Christmas, when Mother and Father drove up from Connecticut with the Corvette."

Redfield remembers too. He twines their fingers together, brings her hand across the table, their hands resting with the food.

Redfield remembers that weekend for other reasons. The next morning his father tapping on the water glass telling him he was going to college whether he liked it or not, telling him he was going to sell the farm.

He brings her hand to his face, slowly holds her fingers to his forehead, his eyes, cheeks, nose, chin, takes them into his mouth.

"You're making me wet," she whispers. "Sucking on fingers. You shouldn't do that. I can feel it all the way down to my crotch."

Redfield lets her hand go, blinks his eyes.

"Don't make fun of me," she says.

"Eat."

After they finish and the restaurant is ready to close up for the night, they pay and cross the street. Redfield watches her walk, the way she moves inside her faded jeans, the cut-outs like windows. Her body looks to be liquid, her white hair fluid.

In the room, Redfield gets his boots off and stretches out on one of the beds in dim blue light. He's too tired to move again. He's been riding against a wall of air for ten hours. He's arm sore and wants the humming that runs from his fingers to his shoulders to cease and desist. He can't tell if his ribs hurt because they've hurt for so long. He thinks about his father in the hospital but can't hold the thought.

Juliet comes out of the bathroom and strikes a pose. She's wearing one of her skirts and a white ribbed T-shirt.

She looks in the mirror and touches her hair back. She's wearing a beaded barrette, red and green and black flecks of light against her white hair.

He comes up behind her and, so quickly it makes her gasp, he has his hands up under her T-shirt and he's palming her naked breasts.

"That feels good," she says, "but you know it's a big no-no."

"You know I know you know . . ."

"Round and round," she says, and that's what he slowly does with his hands.

"No. I meant what you said about knowing."

He gets one of his hands on her ass and rubs it as if the skirt will shine like polished wood.

"Are we going to do this?" she asks, her head thrown back.

"Who are you asking?"

"I don't know. You, I guess."

She moves back into him and reaches behind her. Her head thrown back and her face turned toward his face, he can feel her unbuttoning his jeans.

"Redfield, damn. You got an erection. That's wonderful."

"Really?"

"It feels like a nice one."

They begin to kiss. He's kissing her. He's kissing her eyes and cheeks. He's kissing her hair and chest. He backs her down onto the bed. He's licking her skin, her ears, her arms and legs. He's letting his saliva pool on her belly and licking it dry. They kiss as if they are discovering they have mouths, as if they are feeding, her head back, neck bridging on the bed, shoulders fluttering.

Her hand comes up and takes his forearm, drags it down to her waist, where she stuffs his hand inside her underpants where she's wet and slick. She gasps again.

"At least one of us should know better," he says.

She unsnaps his denim shirt and kisses his chest, moves her mouth to his ear and makes it wet, breathes on it as if only he were someone who could hold her like air and water, hold her gently, let her sift through like sand.

He can't get enough of her body and it's because it's a body. It sighs with life. It's human, similar and different to his own. You touch and it touches back and that touch makes fusion, tells you you're alive too.

He thinks: I want to slide my arms around you, against your skin, inside your skin. I could be your skin.

Her milk begins to come and he drinks it.

"Redfield," she says. "I want you to take my breath away."

She pushes him onto his back and pulls down his jeans. She pulls the crotch of her underpants aside and settles down, surrounding him, all, all around him. She rocks her hips feeling him inside her and it's hot and wet.

He thinks: This is my life.

She thinks: This is my life.

She stays on top of him even though she doesn't belong there, crashing, breaking gravity. Maybe she's as whole and even as the ocean from outer space. Maybe she's as still and constant as light from dead stars. Maybe she's moss . . . She feels him slipping from her, sees the sadness come across his face.

"Oh," she says. "I think I tipped over."

★

She lies beside him, keeping his hand clenched between her legs. She moves her lips over his ear, sucks on a strand of his hair.

"I thought I was going to die," she says.

"No. Nothing like that. Or were you talking about something else? A different time?"

"I have decided that from now on when I make love to someone, it'll be someone who I would not mind if they killed me."

"That kind of raises the stakes."

"It's the times. It's the consequences of making love."

He slowly turns his hand between her legs. She traces his face with her finger, telling him he's getting better, telling him he was wonderful, telling him it'll just take a little time. She makes noises in her throat. She reaches down and feels how he's still soft, so she rides his hand, rides his leg and she can't get enough of him.

*

"We'll have a son," he says, "and we'll name him Earth."

She laughs, taken by the idea. She's proud of him for being so dumb about love and hope and dreams. About children. Dumb as a stump. Dumb as she is in her own true self.

"We'll have a daughter," she says, "and we'll name her Hazel."

They're in the motel pool in the dark and the water is warm, the way water holds the day's heat and slowly gives it up to the night. They're in the deep end, each thinking they're holding the other up.

"That story," he says. "I really didn't tell you the truth."

"My goodness," she says. "What all could you be talking about. You going moody on me. Honesty, why I'd never consider such a thing. Which story?"

"Don't make fun."

"I'm sorry. Which story?"

"It was my baby. I was the father. I got her pregnant. She was my girlfriend for a little while."

"I think I kind of knew that."

"I stopped to see her before I came West. I wanted her to take me in and make everything go away. She said, You're only having a moment of weakness. I looked at her. I thought, I could've loved her."

"You hardly knew her."

"I know."

They float in the water, displacing it wherever they go, buoyant in this medium, nothing between them.

"I'm sorry about your baby," Juliet says.

"I'm sorry about yours," Redfield says.

They've come here to rest. They've come here to be away. They've come here for reasons and they don't know what they are. They've come here because it's a place to come to. No matter. It's hard being. It has to do with how all reckonings stand in the past, how we can only realize what we've done and not what we'll do, but if you have enough pieces it will look whole.

It has to do with how you can collapse your life into moments like: I'll always remember my birthdays. I've had the best life because I've had the best birthdays. I sleep so well at night. Maybe that was the son I was going to have and he came early. Sometimes I want to kill myself; not often enough, but close.

Juliet drizzles a handful of water onto his head, tells him, "Look, a shooting star."

Redfield finds the last glimpse of the star before it disappears in the mountains.

"Do you think we should shoot back?" he says.

★

For a moment he takes in the sun. Then he goes back inside and she's dressed, her satchel on the bed. She's settling the phone back into its cradle. He comes up behind her and gets his thumbs in her belt.

"Nobody home," she says, letting her head go back. They sway and breathe together, his air short and even, hers slow and measured. She turns to face him, wraps him in her arms and pulls his head down onto her shoulder.

"It's okay," she says, stroking his neck. "You're just a red-blooded American boy and I'm a red-blooded American woman. So what if we share some of the same red blood."

"Yes," he says. "So what."

They get gone on a run that will take them four hundred miles. Redfield doesn't want to stop but for gas and then only to avoid her in those moments. He doesn't want to talk, because he's almost due north of New Mexico, passing over its southern lie. To talk would only give sound, life, to what they both know is just over the curve of the earth.

On a four-hundred-mile run through the Empty Quarter, sagebrush country, canyons. The Spanish came here to find gold, the Mexicans came for slaves and the trappers came for beaver. They ride through the bract aster, glimpses of red rock, cottonwoods, rusted trailers, explorer's gentian, blue gentian, yarrow. Dinosaur country. Dry sloughs.

At Vernal they cross the Green River and the Yampa running low and warm. They ride through the land of gray-green sagebrush, high rolling plateau country, this land in the rain shadow of the high mountains, renegade storms traversing the desert. There are grazing cattle and sheep, grain and hay, irrigated alfalfa.

Mostly there's emptiness. Redfield thinks he could live here, maybe in a high slender valley in sight of a lake, an earthen amphitheater of gentle meadows, a lake scooped from bedrock or formed when moraines blocked ice melt.

Along the Green and Yampa rivers, Canadian geese, blue herons, turkey vultures and peregrine falcons live by air, by water, by land.

They stop to eat. Redfield buys bread and a stick of pepperoni. Juliet buys fruit and water. They share their food, sitting closer, handing it over, feeding it into each other's mouths.

"You've been avoiding me," she says.

"No, nothing like that."

"My misunderstanding."

"We'll stop in a while. Somewhere near Steamboat."

At night they collapse on the bed. So tired. Another motel. Another state. Windstruck. Waterstruck. Sunstruck. This one a motorcourt. This one Colorado.

"What color are your underpants?" he says.

"White."

"Good."

She gives him the finger and he notes how long it is, how slender. He holds her hand and turns it, wanting to see the finger from all sides. He slips it in his mouth, where she lets him keep it. He thinks of the white patch between her legs, the promised land.

"You're going glassy again. You've got that hazy look in your eyes."

"It's your beauty," he says.

"I appreciate what you're saying, but I'm not all that beautiful."

"To me you're a goddess, the Statue of Liberty, Miss Venus U.S.A., Marilyn Monroe all wrapped in one."

"Miss Venus U.S.A.?"

"Yeah, you know, Miss Venus U.S.A."

"I guess so."

Inside her faded jeans, she moves like liquid again. He thinks he could eat the rivets off those jeans. The four-letter C-word thrums in his brain. A mantra. He watches her undress, jacket, chaps . . . If there is anything he wants in life, it's never to get over the sight of a woman skinning off a pair of blue jeans.

He thinks how far they've come. How far to go.

He starts to lick her, feels the muscles in her legs flex and release. He wants to lick down to her bones. He wants to possess her, make New Mexico something forgettable. She holds his head and strokes it as if to coax more current into her body. But this doesn't go like silk, like ice, like salve, like nitro. Too long on the road. The head full of too many wrongs. Beginner's luck used up in Utah. It's more like work. Her pelvis quakes. Her stomach goes to ridges. Her chest is awash with sweat and milk and her head begins to ache. Redfield's jaw feels swollen and there are moments when he thinks he's drowning. She begins to pant and her eyes roll back in her head.

When it's over, her body goes slack in the dark room and he collapses, his cheek on her belly. They rest on the edge of breath until their bodies go quiet and their sweat cools in the dark machined air.

Redfield gets on his hands and knees. He dips his head to her belly and kisses her skin. It's slick and tastes coppery. He swabs at the wetness on his face and asks if she's okay. Tells her not to look, but thinks it's her time of month.

"It was like getting stabbed with a rusty knife," she says, "only good, I think."

"I think I get it."

He pinches her and she makes a squealing noise.

"Don't," she says. "I'm helpless."

She can't move, can't laugh, feels like jelly. She pets his head and says, My little hero. Redfield swabs at his face again and turns on the light by the bed. Its whiteness goes off in his eyes. In his vision there are hundreds of tiny basketballs bouncing off his forehead at odd angles.

"Don't look," he says, falling off the bed, getting up and staggering into the bathroom for a towel.

But she does look. She rises up on her elbows. Between her legs the sheets are soaked in blood. Her torso and thighs have been mopped red and glisten in the electric light.

"It's you," she yells. "Not me."

She hears him fall and runs in to find him on the linoleum, passed out, his nose pumping blood.

"It's you," she whispers. "Your nose."

★

He wakes in darkness, cool fingers, a cloth on his forehead, one hand in an ice bucket. He thinks how the cloth must be white. Ice is frozen water. The fingers are Juliet's. He is okay. Juliet is like a nurse.

"We should go back."

"Shhhh," she says. "Shush now."

Her breath is minty. Her fingers are cool. She feeds him water.

"We should go back East."

"I can't go back," she whispers. "My life is out here now."

"We'll go back. Go back together. Go home for the fall just to see the leaves."

"You can never go home."

"Home is where the heart is. There's no place like home. We'll live on the farm. We'll make it all better. I love you."

"Yeah right. Junkie love."

"It won't be forever. I am very thirsty."

She feeds him more water. He can see the other bed's been stripped. Sheets are draped over the furniture, drying in the room.

"It wouldn't be forever," he says.

"No. Drop me in Denver and I can fly back to Albuquerque. I thought it was a decision I had to make, but it never really was. It was something I always knew I'd have to do."

He sits up and takes another drink. He feels as if he could drink a case of something, anything. He swings his feet onto the floor, drinks again and stands up. He walks the room. His legs are new and he's not sure of them yet. His ribs begin to hurt as if the pain takes a little longer to wake up, and he's relieved. Her smell and feel is on him and it seems to catch light wherever it is. It sparkles on his skin like the glittery scales of a fish, like the colors inside a whelk shell.

Juliet gets up and goes to him, follows him to make sure he's okay. On the table by the window he can see his Colorado and New Mexico maps.

She says these words: "I want to go south."

"It's too late," he says.

"No it isn't. It's never too late."

"That's true, but sometimes it is."

★

That night in Colorado the rain comes like a stampede, like horses crossing the roof, Western horses: palominos, creamellos, Appaloosas, roans, serinas tearing holes in the sky and plunging through them. The sky torn. It cracks. Noise painted in a clap of air.

She wakes up. He's sitting on the edge of the bed watching *The Yearling.* Tears are streaming down his face. She curls up around him and goes back to sleep, her fingers slipped inside his bandages.

When she wakes again and rises up through tenths of wakefulness she hears the Toys singing about how gentle the rain is and outside that's just what it's still doing. The room is suffused with the fragrance of rain. Redfield is sitting at the window talking to himself. He's saying, "So I said and then she said and then I said . . ."

"Come back to bed," she says. "We'll sleep in today. We can't travel anyways."

". . . I travel at night. I like to see the country in the dark. When I travel through your town and you're in bed behind a locked door, think of me. Think of me passing through in the night. I think of you. Vampires live at night. They work the swing shift. Think about how locks are for honest people. How would you be if I broke my hand on your face. Old people turn left into your path. They just don't see you. Blood tastes like a mouthful of pennies. Fear. Huge fear. What is direction when the earth is round?"

He gets up and lies down beside her.

"Redfield. What do you think about when you're traveling?"

"A woman named Muriel Peffer."

"Who is she?"

"I don't know. Someone I just made up."

"Really?"

"Really. I worry about stuff. I worry about all the people in the world who might not like me."

"Do you think there are many?

"I don't know. I mean that. I don't know."

She can tell he's serious. He really means it. He truly does nurture fear.

"What else do you think about?"

"The Fed Ex people in Memphis shuffling through mail that has to go out the next day. I worry about them. Do they have a place to live? Do they have enough food? Are they warm?"

"I imagine they do. They probably make decent money."

"But say what if they didn't make decent money. Say they were just poor people."

"They'd be cold and hungry."

"I know what you think about," he says.

"Yes, you do."

"Is it every night?"

"Every night. Every morning. Every day."

"You know what it says when you come into Pennsylvania?"

"No. What's it say?"

"It says: America Starts Here."

"I don't get it. Do the people in New Jersey know that?"

"I don't know. Maybe that's why they have the sign, so people in New Jersey will know that."

"Maybe it has to do with 1776 and all that."

"Wouldn't it say America Started Here?"

"Yes. I guess it would. We're in America now, aren't we?"

"Yes. Colorado is in America."

"Do you think the sign makers in Pennsylvania know that?"

"I don't know. If they do, they certainly think it starts with them."

"Who cares. History is such a waste of time. Time is too important to be wasted on history," she says. "When I have a child, I'll teach him trust and disobedience."

My plunging mind, she thinks. She reaches down into his pants and holds him.

"You used to have such a little baby dick," she says.

"I'm not a little boy anymore."

"Yes you are. All little boys are little boys. You have breasts," she says, kissing his nipple.

"I know. My chest grew that way from since I was a kid. I'm very strong, but I have no definition in my chest. It used to embarrass me."

"Don't worry. They aren't very big."

"What should I do? Get some implants?"

"No. I meant they aren't something you should worry about. Being a man and all. I think they are attractive. They make you kind of androgynous."

"Something I've always wanted."

"I remember when you used to melt crayons onto your skin. You'd go through a whole box of them."

"I don't remember that."

"Yes. You used to. It was really beautiful."

He rolls over onto his stomach, his face in the pillow. Juliet climbs on top of him. She sits on his ass, her arms out and sinuous. She's thinking about undertow, trying to imagine how it is to drown.

Redfield says, "When I came off the George Washington Bridge, it was like I could see the whole country stretching out in front of me. All three thousand miles of it."

Juliet rides him.

"I was thinking if I could move fast enough, nothing could ever catch up with me, not even time. I could see to the ocean and then I thought I heard someone call my name and then I got lost. Last fall a guy went through campus carrying a cross. He had a little axle going through the back end and little bicycle wheels. I saw him go down the street. I couldn't get it out of my head, so that evening I went out riding and found him down the road sitting on the guardrail. The cross was laid over on its side."

Juliet lies down, rests her head on his back. He can feel her there, light and hot, enough weight to settle his quaky insides. She kneads his flesh, strokes and pets his head.

"So I stopped and the guy says, I don't know if I can go on. Well, it's your cross to bear, I say. He looks at me and says, We'll cross that bridge when we get there. Don't get cross with me, I say. We're both laughing. The guy tells me he's dragging this cross to Florida. So I say, Get on the back and we'll go to Maryland. We got down the road a ways and a trooper stopped us because we were towing an unregistered vehicle. The cross wasn't registered. We got to laughing really hard. The trooper, too, and he let us go."

"That's good," she says, petting him some more.

"This other thing I remember," he says, rolling over with her rising up to stay on top. "Sit lower," he tells her, and she settles onto his thighs.

"Is that better?"

"Now, this is very important. One night I was running the interstate and way off I could see light towers, big banks of lights, and I thought it was a prison. But it wasn't. Way off I could see bleachers and tiny people. I could see it all. It was a baseball game. I knew there were people there. Men on the field and people watching who love them. It's a hot night and there's lemonade and Pabst and hot dogs. It was like being in America for the first time. It really was."

And then he stops talking because he's gone hard and she has taken him inside her and he thinks this might be the time it all works.

★

Redfield wakes up. For the second time in two days he's hungry and thirsty. He knows he must eat and drink. He slips out of bed and dresses. He goes down the street and buys food: croissants and beef jerky, cheese, pickles, Pepsi, chips, ham. He fills his basket with whatever he thinks will taste good: chocolate bars, cashews, pepperoni. He buys colorful food: Gatorade, fruited Jell-O, mustard. He buys health food: refried beans, broccoli, wine and a six-pack.

He stands in line and listens to people talk . . . So the guy had all this bridgework done and I smashed him in the mouth. Now there's a bench warrant out there for me. He wants to sue me, but you can't get blood out of a stone.

He pays for his food and goes back to the motorcourt. She's there at the door waiting for him when he comes in. She socks him in the eye and starts to cry.

"Don't you ever leave me again. Don't you ever leave me like that. I told you before."

"It's all right," he says, his eye watering. "It's all right."

He sets down the bags and lies back on the bed, his forearm across his eyes. She brings him a cold cloth.

"Damn," he says. "That kind of hurt."

"I'm sorry, but I warned you not to leave without telling me."

Juliet sits by the window. She has the curtains open and stares out at the gray wet sky.

Redfield gets up after a while and collects his groceries. He puts a towel down on the table in front of her. He makes sandwiches out of croissants and beef jerky. He opens the pickle jar and breaks out the chips. He pours drinks and slices cheese. Juliet says thank you and begins to eat in small bites.

She says, "Do you know what that asshole said to me the first time he met me?"

"No. What?"

"Oh, Juliet, like in the movie. He thought *Romeo and Juliet* was a fucking movie."

"Not such a huge mistake for your average bear."

"Don't you ever say anything nice about him. I need you to hate him too, so in case I run out of hate, yours will spill over into me. I should have known better. He was just a New Age creep. Said he had this wounded child inside him. Fuck him."

"He said to tell you he wants you back. He said if that's how your spirit flows."

"Tell that guy if you ever see him again to kiss my ass."

"My father said there was a moment in time when we could choose between beauty and ugliness and before we could decide, the law came down and ugliness chose us. That's his version of history. He said our names Romeo and Juliet were just a crazy thing they did at the time."

Juliet opens her mouth to speak, but before she can, Redfield puts food inside it.

★

When it's dark Juliet makes her face up. She turns to Redfield, her face is white, her lips red, and she says she wants to go out, to be amongst people in Colorado.

They go down the street and find a quiet joint. There are puzzles on the tables, coils of steel that need to be separated, knot tricks, square pegs that need to go through round holes. There's also green chili and Ernest Tubb is on the jukebox. Patsy Cline.

They buy beer. Redfield tells her a story about a guy he knows who came home drunk and passed out with his motorcycle helmet still on. When he woke up it was all dark. His head weighed a ton and he couldn't hear anything. He got up and walked around the house like that until Redfield showed up and asked him why he had his helmet on.

Juliet laughs, her hands like birds just in flight. Still laughing, she bums a cigarette. She holds it like a prop.

Redfield bounces his leg and drums his thumb on the table. He sings along with the music and does his best John Wayne. He needs her laughter. He needs to delight her. She is the sun by day and the moon at night. He is an earth tremor, a bare quake.

The guy Juliet bummed the cigarette from goes, "Hey, sweet lips." She ignores him and he says it again, this time touching her arm.

"Go fuck yourself," she says.

"I'd rather fuck you."

"Don't mess with me, buster. I'm here with Redfield. He'll pull your asshole out through your nose. He's a crazy."

"I'm scared," the guy says.

"You should be. He's a wild-eyed Vietnam vet. He's crazy because there were no parades when he got home. He's whacked out on drugs and heart disease."

Redfield leans over to Juliet. He says, "Don't forget the part where you say, He's killed before and will do it again."

"He's killed before and will do it again."

The guy starts to laugh.

"You two are okay," he says.

"Hey," Redfield says. "You're the guy who smashed out someone's bridgework. There's a bench warrant out on you."

"How do you know that?"

"I heard you in the grocery store this morning. Or was it yesterday. I keep running into people."

"You guys are okay. Where's your ride?"

"Motel, last time I looked."

The guy is from Florida. He's riding a Soft Tail. He read in the paper where there aren't enough cowboys in Montana, so that's where he's headed. He's flying an M.I.A. flag. He flies it for the brothers still in Nam, Laos and Cambodia. His own brother shot down.

"Missing in Action," Redfield says.

"Missing in America," the guy says.

"I should call home," Redfield says.

★

The night has turned warm. Juliet steps off the edge and makes a *fluff* sound as her body knifes the water. Redfield sits down on the pool's edge and eases himself in. There's a sickle moon in the sky. They get their faces close together so they can whisper, conspire like children. She speaks into his cheek. He talks to her eye, his lips brushing her lash. Their pain stays on dry land and they wonder why.

"I think it's because there isn't so much gravity," he whispers.

"For me, I think it's because deep in my brain I'm reminded of being a fetus. There's that fetus memory."

Redfield sighs. He had himself convinced there was no such thing.

"Oh no," she says. "I'm sorry. It's not like you have it as a fetus. It comes afterwards. It starts at birth. Memory, I mean."

They float to the end, where the wine bottle sits under the diving board. In the board's shadow she takes a sip and then another. She holds it and kisses him, letting the wine seep into his mouth.

"That's nice," he says, and feeds her a drink from his mouth.

They share the wine this way until they hear a scratching sound that goes to a tapping. They look to see a man with a cane and a towel. He's wearing swim trunks. They stay quiet under the diving board. The man takes off his shirt at the gate, leaves his towel there too and taps his way to the ladder. He slips out of his sandals, collapses his cane and climbs down the ladder. They watch him bob and swim. He floats, does hand stands and somersaults underwater. He stays to the shallow end swimming back and forth inches from the bottom. He's dark and shadowy, quick as a swallow. He comes up for air and goes back down again, touching off the sides, planting his feet and surging forward.

The man gets out and towels himself dry. He finds his sandals, shirt and cane. He snaps his wrist and the cane whips out to length. Redfield wants him to say something, to say goodnight. He wants to think the man knew they were there all along, and maybe he does, but he gives no sign. He taps and scratches the cane on the walkway, making his way out of sight.

Juliet whispers, "I feel like a spirit or a soul. One and the other."

★

When she wakes Redfield is sitting at the table drinking coffee from a Styrofoam cup.

"Miss Juliet," he says. "I snuck out and got coffee. I hope you don't mind. I left you a note."

He points to the mirror with his coffee cup. In soap it says, Gone for coffee. Just a minute.

"The world is full of color today. Post-rain color. Redolent. I can smell you and the smell is reminiscent. Today's words are *redolent* and *reminiscent*."

"I'm glad you got back before I woke up. I'd hate to be alone. I'd be pissed."

"Have to punch me again."

She knows that today they part in Denver. She can tell it's on his mind. He's cheerful in a sad sort of way and she's the opposite.

"Redfield," she says. "You have your boots on the wrong feet."

"Come with me," he says.

Out of Steamboat Springs, Route 40 drops south, then east again toward Denver. Like smoke jumpers they descend through the valley fog. Juliet holds to his back, her legs slung over his thighs. From Denver she'll fly to Albuquerque and face what? She doesn't know. In the time before, she thought about killing herself, thought about long sharp lines revealing her arm's interior, her blood mixing with cold bathwater, wings of it like birds of paradise, the mixing of mediums, wandering dimensions. This is the secret imagining that women must carry.

She thinks, No, not now. Now I am a mother and have responsibilities. But then again when all else fails, some alternatives cannot be ignored. It is the passion that compels me and can defeat me. Can we talk about this? Absolutely not. Inside the word *therapist* lurks the word *rapist*. Once you see that word, you can see no other.

She works her right hand between the buttons of his shirt. Life is a sinking ship, but it ain't women and children first. What about Lorelai? What *about* Lorelai? Now she's a mother. I'm really very sorry, Lorelai, but I am left with these huge breasts, left in the blue days. I am left looking for something I can't find, looking for estrogen alone.

He drives on and it begins to rain. Juliet squeezes him at the waist and he flinches. She gets her mouth up to his ear.

"Look for a bridge," she says.

He keeps driving. She tucks her head into his back and the rain doesn't touch her. And then the rain stops just as quickly.

In Kremmling they cross the Colorado River and pick up Route 9 to Frisco, trimming along the Blue River. When they hit I-70, Redfield goes west instead of east to Denver. Juliet holds her breath, giving no indication of knowing the change in his plans. She reaches to his neck and strokes his ear.

They follow I-70 a few miles, traversing the spine of the Rockies, and then pick up Route 91 at Tennile Creek and drop south to climb Fremont Pass at eleven thousand feet. It's cold as hell. What was a spit of rain is now snow. The road before them is gray and, in front of that, silver and watery with light. It stays out in front of them, slick and cold, and that's what he's driving toward, that spot she's afraid she'll never get to.

Redfield pulls over in the thin air so they can get more clothes on. There's snow in the mountains. Again to stand on the land, to stand so high is to confuse your worth. But here the altitude takes your air. A hand closes on your chest. He begins to breathe deeply, struggling to pull out his leathers, another shirt, rain gear. They get on more layers of clothes, one arm at a time, one leg at a time.

He holds out as long as he can and then he starts to cry. Tears on his cold red cheeks soaking his face.

"What's the matter," she yells.

"I have to piss," he screams, "and I have all these clothes on."

Shaking, he crosses over the guardrail. Stiff-legged, he takes three steps forward and drops from sight, disappearing off the road bank. He slides to the bottom, pulling handfuls of grass.

Juliet goes down and helps him up. He's wet his pants and for the first time she sees the red stains. She mops her face with the back of her hand. She coos to him. She gently helps him back to the road.

They keep on south through Leadville, Buena Vista, Salida, the Arkansas River running out on their left and the University Mountains to their right, Mt. Harvard, Mt. Yale, Mt. Princeton. There's a storm coming from those mountains, warm weather from the west through the blue gray sky, smoky at the cloud edges.

In Monte Vista they cross the Rio Grande and she can feel its water running through her, lapping at her, beckoning her. It's telling her to follow, to come along and be quick about it.

As far as Redfield goes, he made up his mind a long time ago.

CHAPTER

They stop for gas in Antonito.

Juliet says to watch for Route 64 out of Tres Piedras. They're running south alongside the Carson Forest. The sign comes and they veer off east over two-lane blacktop, silver gray in the sun. Outside Taos they cross the Rio Grande again and again she feels its pull, stronger and deeper, its draw turning her inside out. Here the Rio Grande cuts a gorge through layers of basalt, a fluid volcanic rock spewed north five million years ago. It ran and ran for many miles, liquid molten fire. These land-slide blocks. The river was larger then. Now it's deeper.

*

Clipping over the gorge 650 feet above the river at 70 mph, Redfield dares to look down.

He realizes that the river doesn't run through the gorge. The river makes the gorge. It's a whole different way of looking at life, and in her own way Juliet is thinking, I will act. I will act. I will do something. She has no idea what, but now the thought courses through her, making her arms and hands and legs strong. She settles back and sets her heels on his thighs, back into the land of scarlet chilies drying in the sun.

*

Juliet rented a car and came to Taos after the baby was born. She came as a way of disabusing herself of her old life, thought the light she'd heard so much about could make her kind of blind. To be with artists. To be an ascetic. But came to feel foolish. It wasn't the colony she expected. It was Newport or Saratoga, maybe Charlottesville. It was the Keys.

That was okay for a while. She could be an art bum, a performance artist, shave her head, or at the very least chop at her hair with a knife and speak in accent, pretend to be Euro trash. She could be a culture whore, be hip, learn what's happening in her time, carry her pain as an affectation, waitress. She didn't last but a day and now she's come again, fancying her strength to be growing like a mountain.

Redfield wonders where he is. They're parked on Paso Del Norte. And while he's at it, he wonders where he's supposed to be. Maybe college? Maybe summer school making up for lost time. *Don't worry, Father—look at it this way. Think of all the schools I haven't dropped out of.* Juliet's in a coffee shop getting some food. Across the street people are surrounding a woman in a Rolls Royce Silver Spirit II. The woman is the color of caramel, black hair, black eyes, and the Rolls is milk white. She won the car at bingo. It's worth $140,000. She won it using heads-up pennies for good luck.

Juliet brings out coffee and sweet rolls. She's wearing a black baseball cap with red hammer and sickles around the crown. Redfield tells her what he's heard from across the street.

"That's wonderful," Juliet says. "Lucky her."

"Yeah," Redfield says. "lucky her."

He starts to smile and be cheerful. He didn't have an opinion up to that point, but now he does, lucky her.

"You know," he says, "I was thinking. I do this thing where I say I have to be somewhere. So I write down a time and I forget whether it's the time I'm supposed to be there or the time I'm supposed to leave so I get there on time."

"Well, always assume it's the time you have to be there and you'll never be late."

"Oh, Juliet, that's good. I knew you'd figure it out. I just knew. Now, what will we do when we get there?"

She looks away, gives off a deep sigh. He eats some

sweet roll and burns his mouth on the coffee. His fall in Colorado smartened him up. He trusts his father to be okay and would want him to be here for Juliet.

"Juliet," he says. "Can I have your baseball cap?"

★

They drive on out of town, taking the high road. They climb the swoop of switchbacks. She knows where she wants to go. She's touching his thigh and pointing. They climb high to the timberline, where the air is rich with the scent of pine resin. Some mountains are green. Some are gray. Some are blue and some are in the clouds. Black-eyed Susans cluster beside the road, congregations of blossoms as big as your hand.

They pass through Truchas. High mountain cemeteries surrounded by picket fences, bedecked with profusions of flowers, ribbons and ornate crucifixes. Desert arroyos, mesas and gullies. This is the land of the Penitentes, the secret men who spike themselves to the cross.

Blocks of basalt and sandstone, great islands of rock, chunks of obsidian. Free range country. Here and there a cattle guard, a wooden aqueduct, a patch of corn, horses and rusted pickup trucks. No matter what, all so tiny, all so insignificant in its occupation of this land coughed up from a volcano, open land, land that already shoulders so much sky.

In Chimayo is a church, ninety by thirty, with walls three feet thick. The nave is continuous. In a pit in a chamber to the left of the main altar is a hollow of earth that contains great medical powers. It can cure the pains of rheumatism, sadness, sore throat, paralysis, and is particularly useful during childbirth.

Pilgrims carry back tiny bottles and handkerchiefs of it. They leave behind crutches, canes and prostheses, wooden legs, plastic hands. They leave flowers, candles, ID papers, photos for the Santos. For Santiago they leave bridles, quirts and sombreros. They leave baby shoes because the Santo Niño travels through the countryside at night and as a consequence wears out his own.

She makes him pull over. He kills the engine and listens to it tick. He can smell the hot transmissions of all who've made this climb to Santuario de Chimayo. She tells him to wait for her while she goes inside the church. There is an outdoor chapel behind the church, stone benches, stone altar.

She goes inside and of a sudden all is quiet. She sits for a while, the peacefulness wicking through her body. She will stay here until it seems to be time to leave. She'll watch the men and women and children. She'll shift in her seat, be comfortable, try to pray, and then she'll go to the sacristy, the healing room, and dab herself with clay from the small pit, collect some in a handkerchief, offer promises, but not yet. Not for a while.

He buys burritos and a Pepsi at Leona's lunch stand, walks down back to the benches. A stream, the Rio Santa Cruz, runs half moon around the chapel and across the stream, the buff Sangre de Cristo Range. Redfield sits down and takes a bit of food.

"I want to be fast and loose, last and foose," he says. And then he fastens on his headphones, gets between stations, lies down and naps in the cool shade, to the sound of static, his wrists crossed on his chest, the sleep of a dead man waiting for pennies to be settled onto his eyes. He's waiting for her, away from the peddlers selling Bultos, saints in wood, and Retablos, saints in paint. Away from the crucifixes, death carts, sacred bones, medals, millagros, postcards and texts.

"We are two birds on the wind," she says.

Redfield thinks, Yes, as still as memory, the quick and the dead.

"I've thought about us for a long time," he says.

"Ray, I can't play with you anymore."

He bolts out of sleep and sees her sitting by him. He thinks, It still could be a dream. Breathe, he tells himself, trying to open his throat to make way for words.

"I've been thinking a long time about rivers," he says. "Connecticut, Susquehanna, Canada, Mississippi, Seneca, Rio Grande, Clinch, Vermillion, Green, Pecos, Colorado. Would you grow your hair down to your ass if I asked you? For me. If I said, For me. I'm treading water, you know."

"Something has to change," she says.

"I want to see the bomb," he says, and she tells him, Okay, he can see the bomb.

She holds a sprig of sage to his face and tells him to breathe.

Down the road they stop and she buys a Two Grey

Hills blanket. She points out an odd thread that exits the pattern through the dark border.

"They weave it into the blanket," she says, "so their spirits can escape the work. It's called a spirit line. Some people say it's a myth, but I believe it."

"I believe what you believe," he says.

Out of Española he follows the signs for Route 30, the Los Alamos Highway. They make for altitude, again to go light-headed in the changing blue, the reds and ochers, the greens and shadow blacks. Settling on the color of things and by then it's become something else, something it will never be again, off by seconds of shade and increments of growth, weather-wearing rock and wind, arranging sand and tuff, particle by particle. We don't belong here, she thinks, on this earth.

They ascend through the life zones: creosote and yucca to aspen to spruce. Switchbacks and long runs, like pinball, like Chutes and Ladders. After a while, they can see Los Alamos up through the canyon, high mesa, high rock. They're running late in the afternoon against the day traffic coming down. At the top of the plateau is a playground and benches, a sign that says: GREEN FORESTS OFFER MORE.

"More what," Redfield yells. "More fucking what."

"Whatever," Juliet says, but her words clip off in the wind.

There are houses and streetlights, hedges and tennis courts, the Trinity Bakery, Oppenheimer Street, ponderosa pine that have seen it all. Churches, churches, churches.

At a stoplight, Redfield says, "Juliet, look. Another beautiful woman. Big tits and all. They must be drawn to such power. Maybe it's the altitude. It makes their breasts swell up. Maybe it's radioactivity. I can't wait to see the bomb."

"I think you're right. I can feel mine swelling as we speak."

"There's another one. Look."

"Now, she's definitely not beautiful."

Parked beside them, a guy and a girl in a convertible listen. What do they think? They think, How exotic, how strange, how these two probably have been or should be arrested. It's a natural kind of feeling.

*

Redfield wants to take the tour. He pulls on his new baseball cap and they go inside. It is a high-tech tour. People are sitting at monitors listening to words and music, mouthing the words. There are A-bomb toys, and comic strips: *Learn How Dagwood Splits the Atom*. People wear fanny packs and plastic pouches in their breast pockets. They carry eyeglasses and calculators, mechanical pencils and ballpoint pens. On the whole they are tall, white, intent people.

Juliet loses him in the maze of displays. She walks between the walls of blue plastic and gray fiberboard. Press a button and monitors flare to life. Numbers, signs, circles, ellipses and floating dots carry all the information.

There's Little Boy. He looks like a fish, a bottom feeder bloated and benign. That's needed in this life. *An atomic bomb is detonated by bringing together very rapidly two subcritical masses of fissionable material. The ensuing explosion produces great amounts of heat, a shock wave, and intense neutron and gamma radiation.*

That's kind of neat, she thinks. I'll have to tell Redfield when I find him . . . if I remember to, if I don't panic.

But this panic. She feels it flying up from her gut, running cold over her ribs. Her breathing quickens and her palms are wet. This is panic, she thinks. Panic at altitude. I know this. I know this. If I know this, why is it fucking me up? She curses Redfield. Where is he? When I find him, I'll kill him.

Still looking for Redfield, but she can't find him. She keeps a hand in her pocket, clutching a leather pouch she carries. Her sweaty palm makes it wet and thick. She walks in on a movie, but it seems out of focus. The words and movement aren't in synch. She lets her body list to one side, cocks her head, tries to make it all be more than a plane of light.

She works her way back to the door. She can see in the visitor book at the door where he's scrawled *fuck Dagwood, fuck Blondi,* and outside the door she can hear the Harley pulling rpms on the clutch. It's trumpeting in the thin hot air, calling to her and he's sitting there, he's crouched over the buckhorns, his cap on backward. She runs to him and gets on behind, just enough time to lock her hands at his waist and they're making for the gate, making for the narrow mountain roads.

Route 502 because it takes him up. She pounds on his

back and screams for him to slow down, tells him he'll kill them.

"I have to get away," he says. "I have to get gone."

They see signs: EXPLOSIVES TRUCKS. Tall stiff spike pines. Deer crossings. She knows she can't do anything. She prays to God.

The road ends and he locks up the wheels, keeps the plunging front wheel aligned with the dragging rear tire. She slaps his right thigh. He goes right, hot on the throttle, still climbing, gaining all the time the sharp switchbacks. Sign: 15 MPH GRAVEL ON ROAD, but he doesn't slow down. Off her left shoulder she sees forever. She sees forever mountains, forever valleys, tops of trees. She sees from Washington, D.C., to Baltimore or, say, from Chicago to Milwaukee, Boston to Hartford, from the earth all the way to the friggin' sun.

They're in the dark blue-green mountains of the Jemez at ten thousand feet, trimming along the rim of the Valle Grande Caldera, the guts of which they've been riding for hours.

What finally stops him is three girls in a little sports car with a flat tire. He passes and pulls over, tells Juliet, "I got a flash for you, Gordon. Get it, Flash Gordon? What's the Mather, Cotton? Get it? Cotton Mather."

"Go change the tire," she says, lying back on their gear, her boot heels on the instruments. It's okay now, she thinks.

Redfield helps the girls change their tire. One is in tie-dye, one in pink and one in black. Every time they bend over he sees down the neck of their tops. Every time he sees down their tops, he looks over to Juliet. She's watching him.

"Is that your girlfriend?" the one in tie-dye says.

Redfield's mind rifles through the words *girlfriend, wife, mother, cousin, sister, friend, girl.* It keeps going while he talks.

"I don't know," he says. "We just came from where they made the bomb."

The girls laugh.

"What so funny?" he says.

"The look on your face," the one in pink says. "You were really thinking. I'll bet she's your girlfriend."

"Yeah," Redfield says, palming lug nuts. "Something like that."

"Where are you two going?" the one in black says.

"I don't know. We're just out and about. Touring."

"Are you from Philadelphia?" tie-dye says. "You got a PA tag. I'm from Philadelphia."

"No. But I love your cream cheese."

The girls laugh some more and he can tell it's the kind of laugh where they think he's funny. Not what he says, but him. He thinks for a second about throwing the lug nuts into the bushes. Remembers an old story his father tells about a guy who loses his lug nuts down a storm drain next to the loony bin. From a barred window he hears a voice go, Take one lug nut from each wheel and that will get you to a service station. That's brilliant, the guy says. The voice goes, I may be crazy, but I'm not stupid.

Redfield wonders if the girls would figure it out. Wonders if their fathers told them stories like that just in case it happened to them, in case they lost their lug nuts or went crazy or had a crazy guy change their tires.

"She's very beautiful," the one in black says. "Your girlfriend."

Redfield motions for them to come closer. They take steps. He gestures them even closer, and they bend down.

"She's my cousin," he says. "She gave up her baby for adoption in Albuquerque and we're going to go take it back."

"No way," the one in pink says.

"Yes. It's a true story."

"Really?"

"Yes. We've slept together too, in Utah, but it wasn't my baby. Is that bad?"

"I don't know," tie-dye says.

"Are you women teachers or students or nurses or something like that? I know you're not nuns."

"No. We're just friends. We're out driving around too. We're kind of like tourists," the one in pink says.

"Be careful," Redfield says, spinning lug nuts, reefing on the lug wrench. "Be careful."

He tells them they should keep his secret and at the same time learn to make wise decisions. He asks the one in tie-dye if she has any smoke or speed. Pharmaceuticals?

"No," she says. "I just dress this way. What's this bomb you were talking about?"

He adjusts his baseball cap and shrugs.

"Just a bomb," he says, and tells them goodbye.

He walks back to Juliet. She's smiling.

"I had to do that," he tells her. "I had to be the Good Samaritan."

"Oh you're just another kid trying to get right with God because you're afraid of the A-bomb."

"Yes. I suppose I am."

Heights of land. Gaining altitude. They stop to put on more clothes. The land turns green and to the east there are pockets of rain where the clouds have tagged the mountains. To the west a bath of sunlight on a mesa. Riding Route 4, they skirt the rim of Valle Grande Caldera, 176 square miles of green meadows. It was left behind after the eruption of five volcanos a million years ago.

It goes: Once upon a time there was a volcano here, the largest volcanic peak on the continent. It was twenty-five thousand feet high. The caldera was twelve miles in diameter and thirty-five hundred feet deep. The first explosion opened vents on the northern and eastern faces. Tons of melted rock plumed skyward, spreading a layer of ash as far as Oklahoma and Kansas. Other eruptions spread blankets of burned rock four thousand feet deep over the surrounding plateaus. Twenty-five cubic miles of its guts spewed into the air until finally the top collapsed, the mountain destroying itself. The top is now a valley eighteen miles long, and the Jemez Mountains make up its rim. Fir and aspen forests grow there in the thin, dry, clean air. It was the earth at work on no human scale. It wasn't slow work, not the dragline of a glacier or the file of wind or water. It must have been a hell of a sight to see. Something to trade your eyeteeth for.

They stop here and stay for a time, knowing they are in some special place.

Juliet tells him of her intentions to go back and get her child, something Redfield already figured out. It's getting swiftly dark in the holy land of New Mexico, the land of cliff dwellings like swallow nests.

Redfield doesn't say anything. He lets her talk herself out until she cries a little bit. Then he holds her so tightly there is no light between them.

"I'll take you," he says, and they're gone again, running off the mountain along the Jemez River inside the stacks of high rock walls. The earth turns red and comes the small crowds of houses again. Piñon and juniper, plots of corn, beans and squash.

17

The twilight spreads thin, loses its milkiness to the night as the shadows lengthen and come together. There are new currents in life. Juliet notes the duration of light. Days are almost getting shorter.

Way off, the Sandia Mountains go watermelon pink. Black bears have been descending from the Sandias onto the highways. Quick glimpses of the bosque furled along the Rio Grande, meandering silently through the valley to make the border of old Mexico.

Under the river, under the flares of cottonwood, tamarisk and Russian olive, under the cooled hot-liquid granite

of the Sandias, the falling travertine formations of the
Jemez, under the curly dock, sweet clover, watercress,
scarlet chili peppers, roadrunner, bull snake, black
widow, hermit thrush, adobe, domes of bread ovens,
asphalt, concrete, tempered, AC blocks of Albuquerque is
the fresh water ocean, the aquifer that is the mother
water.

They ride along the ditches, the dusty roads of Corrales. They're coming off a trip, a long run, and no matter
how far they've been, it's a little like coming home because this is where they started, atop the desert ocean.

There's a sign on the door. It says the locks have been
changed. *There is now a security alarm in place. Your stuff is
inside. Call me and I can arrange for you to retrieve your
belongings.*

On the door there's a placard. PINKERTON SECURITY AND
INVESTIGATION.

Redfield is thrilled. He pulls the FOR SALE sign out of the
ground and drives it through the picture window. They
wait for a siren, for horns and bells, but there is no noise.
He rakes the jamb with the signpost, helps Juliet through
and then climbs in after her, cutting his thigh on a shard
of glass still in the frame.

"Get only what you need," he says, holding his hand
to the back of his leg.

She looks at her dismantled table, the furniture draped
in white. She tips over boxes that have her name written
on them, sorts through her belongings with the toe of her
boot, but doesn't find anything.

She goes out the back door and sits in the new darkness where she can still see the mountain. She starts to cry, her tears sliding to her mouth where she can taste them. Two states' worth of wind and salt gone wet like a mouthful of nickels. She feels her resolve scattering away again. She had such faith.

Redfield comes onto the patio, the FOR SALE sign over his shoulder. He smashes the window in the door behind him. He likes the sound of breaking glass.

"I am so afraid," she says, "that I've already had the last good year of my life."

"Hush. How foolish," he says, wandering the patio.

"I love this place. I bet the mountain was blue today."

"Maybe we'll come back sometime."

He pulls up a flagstone and finds a sealed plastic bag containing Texas grit. Strictly high octane. He smiles. It's like a welcoming of evil. He heaves a wrought iron chair through another window and then goes back inside to make coffee.

Juliet stares off at the mountain, counts off the climb in life zones. Grama grass and piñon to ponderosa pine to Douglas fir and quaking aspen to spruce to bald rock.

Up there was the first man, Sandia man, twenty-five thousand years ago. He moved up there because the toposhere loses one thirtieth of its density with every nine hundred feet of altitude gained. It made for 150-mile horizons. He liked the view. He liked to see the curve of the earth. It was safe. He left behind flaked spear points and shaped bones. He was a big game hunter: horse, bison, camel, mastodon. Juliet wonders if Sandia man was a good father. She wonders if Sandia woman was a good mother.

She stays seated in her chair, drifting in the night. I'll just catch my breath, she thinks. I'll be like a recovering drunk, like a recovering addict. I'll take one step at a time, one small step at a time. I'll be Neil Armstrong.

Redfield is inside the house. She can hear him. He's making Redfield noises: clunks and thuds, noises quick and staccato, metal on metal, wood on wood, bone on bone. She smiles: That's her Redfield.

She closes her eyes and clutches at the edges of the blanket. She reaches into her pocket, feels the leather bag, squeezes its fat bottom made full by a handful of earth. In Egypt sometimes the crazy *magnoon* are considered holy. Maybe she could go there to be crazy, to be holy. Redfield would have no trouble. He's already both.

When he comes out, he's dragging her table. His eyes are lit up like pilot light, like afterburners, like rocket's red glare.

He says, "I put your table together rairly fapidly."

She says, "What?"

He says, "Fairly rapidly."

She says, "Burn it."

★

The house is attached to a bluff overlooking the Rio Grande, four descending stories of concrete, steel and glass.

Must've given the architect a hard-on, Redfield thinks. Plenty of grounds and trees called landscaping. There's the chimney for cozy winter nights. There's a tennis court, financial security and hearts to share with your precious gift. Expenses paid, a home filled with love, devotion, warmth, laughter and education.

At the door Redfield stands behind Juliet, resting his chin on the top of her head. He waits for her to make a move but she doesn't, so he does, touching the small white light of the doorbell.

They can hear someone coming, unlocking, turning, opening.

How would you be? After all, this is your greatest fear. Would you remember your manners? Would you have planned for this? Just how full of love, devotion, warmth and laughter would you be? How about relief? Maybe you'd think, Fuck me, and you'd be a lot right.

"You got any warm beer," Redfield says. "I like warm beer."

"You're not supposed to be here," Rick says.

"She wants to feed her baby."

"I want to feed my baby," Juliet whispers.

"You have to leave."

"I can't," she says. "If I don't have my baby, I will kill myself."

"I don't believe this is happening," he says, as if it'd finally come to be and now he's relieved. "Juliet, you're being dramatic."

"Some things you just can't make up," Redfield says.

"Is it money you want?"

"No," she says. She has her knuckles in her mouth and is softly beginning to weep.

"This is against the law," he says. "You made your decision. You're being immature."

She tries to speak, to tell him she's changed her mind, but she can't. The words get caught in her throat and she has to make a choice between speaking and breathing, so she huffs and squeaks.

"What did you say?"

Redfield steps in front of Juliet. His ribs ache as he makes his chest fill his leather jacket, as he rocks forward on the balls of his feet. He wants to be menacing, to be willful, to endanger his species.

"She says she's more worried about sin than the law. Besides, it's America and everybody gets a second chance."

"You have no one. What will you do?"

She points to Redfield. "He's someone."

Lorelai calls from down below. She calls to her husband. She asks who it is. The words come more loudly the closer she gets.

At first she sees Redfield and smiles because she doesn't know who he is. Maybe his car broke down, maybe he's selling something, maybe he's the friend of a friend. She shifts the baby to her other arm.

Then she sees Juliet. Inside herself is a moment of suspension and then she collapses. She feels first her organs going south and then the floor following. The baby seems to flutter in her grasp, seems to be heavy as lead. Desperately, she thinks it's an earthquake, at least a landslide and the bluff is shrugging her home off into the Rio Grande. She hopes for those things.

She says, "My milk didn't come in. We thought it might, but it didn't."

"I'm sorry to hear that," Juliet says, quietly.

Juliet shrugs the blanket off her shoulders and reaches out. She says, "Come here, baby girl. Come here."

They watch her take the baby. She cradles it in her left arm, unzips her jacket and gets the baby to her wet T-shirt, to her breast, to her heart. The baby fixes her eyes on Juliet as she begins to suckle.

"I knew you were coming," Lorelai says. "I knew you were coming." She keeps saying it, says it on her feet, says it in the chair she finds, says it to the floor with her head between her knees.

"Where have you been," Juliet keeps saying to the infant. "Where have you been."

Redfield finds Rick in the kitchen punching numbers on the phone. Without a word, he unfolds his knife and strokes it across the cord.

"Don't do that," he tells Rick, his voice going to gravel, going to panic. He's throbbing inside. Breathe, he thinks. Keep breathing.

"Don't do that," he says, backing Rick to the sink, holding the knife at his hip.

He feels himself going to water, water trickling through his pores, bursting from his forehead, dripping down his back, down his ass and the good ache of pain in his bones coming like a metronome. The kitchen is white tile, white light, fluorescent light. Redfield can feel it to the roots of his eyeballs.

"You're going to *hurt* me?" Rick says, not being able to imagine it could come to this, finding it hard to believe people still did such things.

"No," Redfield says. "But there's something I want to tell you."

Redfield holds up his left hand and tells Rick it's the center of the heart meridian. He tells him not to fuck in the summer because sperm count drops a hundred million in the heat. Tells him to go without underwear. He says, Don't worry. This could happen to anybody. This is probably a bad dream you're having. This is probably a bad dream I'm having. You take chances in life.

Redfield lays the back of his left hand on the counter. He looks at Rick and then stares down at his hand on the white tile. It looks strange to him, dirty and red, clouds of white, lines across lines, threads of blue and purple.

He raises his right hand above his head. He pauses for a moment that is all time and then drives it down, stabbing the knife into his open palm. He sees how his fingers leap to grasp the blade. He makes no sound. He twists, draws back to his wrist. When his hand opens, a red line blossoms and goes to tears. He thinks, Now this is my life.

"That's what I wanted to tell you," he says, his voice thin and quavery, his knees weakening.

When Juliet looks up, Redfield is standing beside her. He's wearing his gloves, wearing his sunglasses. He's saying it's time to go. Rick is beside him, his face gone ashen. He goes to hold Lorelai, to hold her back.

"I want you to keep my table. It's a good table," Juliet says, but then she remembers the table's been burned and she feels terrible about how disappointed they'll be when they find out. "Another thing, too. I think something is wrong with your security system at the other house. It didn't go off."

"I only bought the sign," Rick says.

"Go," Redfield says, nudging her.

Juliet tells him she needs his jacket to wear. It'll be big enough to fit the baby inside.

"Wait," Lorelai says, opening a closet by the door. She takes out a small travel bag. She gives it to Juliet and says, "I won't be needing these anymore."

Rick is staring at Lorelai. She stands under his gaze, turning her head, looking about as if she doesn't know what all is going on, as if she's saying goodbye to an old friend.

Redfield takes Rick by the arm. He says, "Remember what I told you," and then follows Juliet up the walk, the blanket draping her shoulders.

He goes slowly, listening to her coo and purr. He knows there are eyes on his back. His hand feels scalded, feels like the bones are tied in knots. He tries to make a fist, but he can't. He keeps his fingers curled so to hold the buckhorns. His glove is soggy.

Behind him he can hear Rick yelling. He's saying, "Don't think for a second that you're getting away with anything."

He wonders how long Rick will be afraid. Long enough, he hopes. Maybe the rest of his life.

CHAPTER

Juliet can see Sandia Crest off her left shoulder and a little behind her. She'll see it like that at night for many days, long after it's gone. She'll see it no matter where she is. She'll see it by looking back and to her left.

They ride through Albuquerque on I-25, light splashed out to the right and left, party to their leaving.

Now, the small breaking up to the east to make a horizon is the lights of the city. Away from the city lights the sky is not so high, not so far. The stars begin to dart through. They cross a river south of Albuquerque but don't know what it is.

He reaches down and slaps her leg. She knows he did it because she keeps looking back and every time she does, she throws the bike a little. The air is full of sage, nothing but the sage on the wind, nothing but New Mexico on his bare arms and against his chest.

Just keep on going, Redfield thinks. Keep on going. Keep it straight. He can feel what is between them, something small and quiet and barely perceptible. It is a part of Juliet rather than something separate. He feels her thighs at his hips, so strong, stronger than ever.

The stars are above them and below them. The stars come down to earth this night. He wonders, What makes desert? Dryness. Evaporation. The absence of water and that absence precludes its presence. What an odd thought to have. Wish I had a gun. I am such a fool.

Being alone. It's what we all fear the most. For me it's the easiest way to be.

This black night and he's on the longest run of his life. He pleasures in the headache he has. It gives him something to feel. It reminds him of something. Evidence of a brain.

He talks out loud: It would be nice to have just one gun, but I'm trying to grow up. Take my place in society. Breathe fire in my heart. Out there are fleeting views of the river, the valley's narrow greenery. I have responsibilities.

On the road is a sign that says JESUS SAVES.

"You're goddamn right he does," Redfield yells.

The bike wavers and Juliet pinches his leg. She's a

mother again, the infant so tiny inside the jacket she wears. Her left arm cradles. In her right she holds a handful of his shirt. Her tears slide back across her temples.

South. Belen. South. Socorro. Gas in the dark. East is the Cristobal Range, the Rio Grande, Jornado del Muerto, Trinity. South. Truth or Consequences. South. Hatch. South. Rincon.

South. South. South. A Chevron attendant with a mustache that loops into sideburns. He has a Sportster in the garage. Insists that Redfield take a look. Cars come to the pumps. One drifts through and they watch it go. In another are two women from Maine, a mother and daughter. They are young and pretty and have bare arms. Juliet wears her blanket, the baby riding close to her chest out of sight.

Redfield asks for the loan of some duct tape as if it's something you return. He wraps it around his gloved hand, around his wrist and up his arm. He has the attendant tape his hand to the buckhorns, tells him to leave a finger for the clutch and tells him he wasn't here. The attendant rides with the Banditos. He says, Hell is our home; we're only visiting here. It goes without saying.

Juliet watches, aware for the first time that he's wounded.

"Redfield," she says. "Redfield."

He can hear her voice in his head and sees her face in the mirror going to horror. It is almost funny. Beautiful and funny.

He asks about going west to Tucson, but the attendant tells him the weather is coming from there. So they push on toward Las Cruces and then the sky is shot pink with orange coils of clouds. Sharp peaks to the left of Las Cruces.

Redfield can smell cowshit and cut hay. There are orchards. Where have I come to, he wonders in the dark blue morning light. Herefords and holsteins graze beside the interstate.

He yells back and in the wind she hears, *Microwave tower. Car phones kill people.*

The sun keeps on coming. The eastern emerald forest is already lit and the prairies are ablaze. A bird flies alongside them, sharing their cut in the wind. They cross into the nation of Texas and the sky is blackening before them. There's a rest stop ahead, so they pull in for a dry spot, a drink of water, free maps and literature, to change a diaper.

They stay behind the trucks, out of sight. Redfield, taped to the bike, looks at the baby for the first time. He didn't know it was a girl. The baby has eyes for only Juliet, seems to recognize her, seems to be trying to remember, seems to say, My heart has been so empty of you because you weren't there. Hold me. Fill my heart back up.

"Your hand," Juliet says, feeding him water. "Oh, Redfield. What did you do to your hand?"

"Go," he says. "We need to go."

In El Paso, the sharp apexes of the Sierra Madres are now pink. There are aquamarine trailers. This is the shattered orogeny of the Florida Mountains, the horse latitudes, the tail end of the Rockies, a tireless land left scarred and gaping for its ore. Being in El Paso is like being on the edge of the earth. It's as if they are making the earth, only it's the opposite. They are taking it apart.

Now it rains, hard driving gusts of dirty rain bringing to ground what the smelters and cookers and furnaces have given loft. Tires sucking rain like zippers, like buzz saws.

"Find someplace to stop," she yells.

★

They lie on the beds.

When he wakes, Juliet and the baby are still asleep across from him.

They'll head for Mexico, the land of paper flowers, land of the Bible, where the law is the Ten Commandments, where the law is whatever you want it to be.

His hand is a weight.

It's wrapped in a towel full of ice gone to melt. It's white and blue and black, looks like something you'd find in a garden, maybe an eggplant or a gourd, a potato from Bolivia.

He looks at the baby. He can't ever remember taking such notice of a baby. Juliet and the baby lie so still. He expects them to move, waits on a small event, and when it doesn't happen he panics and prods them. They show life and he feels foolish, but thinks the words *you never can tell.*

All at once he's stricken with thirst, fears he'll die for lack of fluids. He gets into the bathroom and guzzles down cup after cup of water. It washes over his tongue and down his throat, sluices over his cheeks, down his neck, and wets his chest. His pains begin to wake up, the hand, the ribs, his knees and the back of his thigh. He tries to remember how he cut the thigh, but he can't. It's going some when you can't even remember how you hurt yourself.

He looks in the mirror and is pleased to recognize himself. He meets his own stare and takes strength as he's bathed in light and heat.

"Ride evil," he says to the mirror. "Never let it ride you."

When he comes out, they are still asleep. On the dresser is her leather pouch. For the first time he sees the contents. There are millagros and fetishes. There's a handful of clay, a crucifix, crystals, sage, obsidian sharp as razor blades and potsherds. Petrified wood. It's her medicine bag.

"Mexico," he whispers. "There will be room for us there."

He looks at the sleeping baby again. It lives in a time-less presence with no past or future. It knows that time is only a way of keeping everything from happening at once. Kind of like Redfield, the way he's trying to escape his life while always carrying it with him.

★

When Juliet wakes it's nighttime. Redfield is asleep in a chair that bars the door, his hand in a bucket of red ice water. He's dreaming: I set out from Pennsylvania in search of Juliet. I was twenty-three when I left and still am. Will always be, because this was the time of my life . . .

"It's time to go," he whispers, his eyes still closed. Breathe, he thinks, breathe.

"Yes."

They dress silently and load their gear on the bike. The rain is somewhere around them, but right here only the pavement is wet. They begin down through the streets, 3rd, 4th, 5th, dropping to the river, passing under the lights. The air like sulphur. The hour is late night, the earliest morning can be. So many people to leave behind. He can see the Stanton Street bridge arching in front of him.

"Free Redfield," he says, fingering the clutch, kicking up the shift. "Free Redfield."

They ride over the bridge of concrete shoulders, over the Rio Grande, his left hand blood-wed to the buckhorns. Into the soft rain, into the south, into Juárez, where they disappear. Free at last. Free at last.

ABOUT THE AUTHOR

ROBERT OLMSTEAD was born in New Hampshire in 1954. His work has appeared in *Black Warrior Review, Granta, The Graywolf Annual 4, Story* and *Louder Than Words.* He is currently writer-in-residence at Dickinson College in Carlisle, Pennsylvania. He is a 1989 recipient of the John Simon Guggenheim Fellowship and the Pennsylvania Fellowship for the Arts. His previous books are *River Dogs,* a collection of stories, and the novels *Soft Water* and *A Trail of Heart's Blood Wherever We Go.*